Death Honk

Nine Tales of the Macabre

JP Mac

Published by Cornerstone Media

Also By JP Mac

Fiction

Hallow Mass
Fifty Shades of Zane Grey
The Little Book of Big Enlightenment

Nonfiction

They Took My Prostate: Cancer-Loss-Hope
Jury Doody

Table of Contents

Dagon and Jill

Santa Monica, CA

Dear Mr. Whateley,

Guiding you through the publishing process would go a lot smoother with email. However, as you insist there's no email in Dunwich, snail mail it shall be. First, congratulations on selling your textbook concepts to the Los Angeles Unified School District. Great timing. The district's religious diversity program, Different Voices, Different Ways, has been on the hunt for nontraditional faiths and yours certainly fits the bill. Mind you, I'm not judgmental. While I have never heard of Cthulhu, Nyarlathotep, or any other Great Old Ones, I'm certain your beliefs are sincere, and your books will contribute to the rich cultural mosaic that is Los Angeles.

To recap: Whitman Press will publish three children's textbooks, based on your creed, for which you'll deliver manuscripts and artwork. The three books are:

> *Dagon and Jill*
> *The Shadow Over Humpty Dumpty*
> *A Children's Necronomicon* (with pop-up section)

As Walt Whitman once said, "I am large. I contain multitudes." Welcome to our multitudes. I look forward to working with you and "opening doors," as you like to say.

Cheers,

      Martin Gelb-Crispling

      Editor

      Whitman Press

PS: I Googled "Dunwich" in north-central Massachusetts. Your town seems to be ground zero for bizarre deaths, livestock mutilations, disappearances, and a host of other mysterious, forbidding events.

All I can say is be careful.

Maybe purchase some pepper spray.

***

Dunwich, MA

Goode Gelb-Crispling,

The stars wheel in their course toward a terrible alignment. Young voices shall call forth that which is ancient beyond time; vital they learn to serve them who dwell in sea, earth, and outer spheres. The powerless crawl before those with it, if ye see my meaning.

Sent ye writing and pictures for first book, *Dagon and Jill*. Will send second book if I am still alive. Last night One that

Dwells Below emerged. Now it roams the hills and has already et up a horse and a lawn goose.

I am yr servant,

Ezra Whateley

***

Santa Monica, CA

Dear Mr. Whateley,

Didn't catch a lot of what you said, but I couldn't agree more about empowering youngsters. Our daughter, Shannon, is being raised to believe she can rule the world.

Going forward, there could be a small problem with *Dagon and Jill* in the chapter where young Jill lures a homeless man out onto a pier, then shoves him into the water. The man is dragged screaming beneath the surface by amphibious monsters, which then reward Jill with a gold tiara covered in seaweed.

This is a wonderful empowerment metaphor about the rewards that come from facing scary things. However, legal is worried some might view it as mean-spirited. Could you include people from other cultures and races, who are also shoved off the pier, so as not to single out the homeless?

Cheers,

Martin Gelb-Crispling

***

Dunwich, MA

Goode Gelb-Crispling,

Yer thought is true. More sacrifices would please Dagon. But Jill is too young to offer so many. Let stand the drawing of the doomed tramp.

Have sent ye words and art for second book, *Shadow Over Humpty Dumpty.* Artwork is mine, drawn in the eldritch light of a gibbous moon. Thing from Below went back down but et up a county road crew. Now police will come again to meddle.

Stars are aligning. Must quickly say the Black Mass and make the Voorish Sign. My youngest boy went mad. He sits drooling on the porch, trying to play the cat like an accordion.

He's been scratched some.

Yer servant,

Ezra Whateley

***

Santa Monica, CA

Dear Mr. Whateley,

Sorry about your son's injuries. That's a problem with cats. You'll be pleased to know Legal withdrew all objections to *Dagon and Jill* after receiving your gift of a sack of gold coins.

They say money talks, but in your case, it hollers through a bullhorn. However, it's not for me to judge.

Our first printing of "Dagon" went out to schools and was incorporated into the Different Voices, Different Ways curriculum. So far, the book has been well received by students and teachers who enjoy the use of fantasy to further appreciation for non-mainstream faiths.

Everyone is delighted.

Except the police.

I don't know if you've heard, but there has been a tragic local incident. Three middle school boys confessed to pushing homeless men off the Santa Monica pier. (Not sure of the total number since no bodies were recovered.) The boys carried *Dagon and Jill* and were caught trying to purchase iPhones with a gold tiara covered in seaweed.

Clearly, this is a case similar to Charles Manson where he used the Beatles' music for criminal ends. Still, I've been unable to determine if we face liability because our entire legal department resigned and moved to Las Vegas, taking along the gold coins. But that's an internal issue.

Still, going forward, there may be more controversial points with your second book, *The Shadow Over Humpty Dumpty*. For example, in one chapter, youngsters Tiffany and Giles ambush and murder a postman. They cut out his intestines and droop them into a 7-11 Big Gulp cup. Late at night, Giles offers the entrails to a round, eerie being seated on a wall. It sips up the guts like spaghetti while Tiffany screams something called, "The Spell of Aklos." (A real tongue twister, which, incidentally, contains no verbs.)

I'm inclined to argue this is a parable telling kids that even with religion there are no easy answers to some of life's problems. Is that correct, or could it be a humorous metaphor on homework? Please clarify.

Cheers,

Martin Gelb-Crispling

***

Dunwich, MA

Gelb-Crispling,

Lad and lass appease the guardian of a doorway. Alter nothing on Spell of Aklos, least ye cause Earth to be dragged into another dimension. And stop ye talking so much. Print what I give ye.

Sending ye words and art for *Children's Necronomicon*. Police broke up Black Mass and chased us, but we lost them in Cold

Springs Glen. Alas, they shot my eldest boy. He died, then dissolved into a puddle o' black stinking liquid.

But I knowed he would, so it's Okay.

Yr servant,

Ezra Whateley

***

Santa Monica, CA

Mr. Whateley,

I don't appreciate your tart tone. We're all trying our best to be sensitive to your religion's eschatology. Once again, our new legal department found no objections to "Humpty Dumpty" after receiving your gift of a large gold bar covered in moss. (You should really consider keeping your money in stocks.) Subsequently, "Shadow" has gone out to schools. Students and teachers are again pleased.

The police, not so much.

Same problem as before, I fear: bad timing. Recently, a half dozen postmen disappeared in Sherman Oaks. One was found dead near a cinderblock wall, split open like a Thanksgiving turkey, intestines missing. Anyway, because the postmen were Federal employees, the FBI stepped in. They questioned everyone at Whitman Press except the legal department, who had resigned and left for Barbados with the gold bar. The FBI seemed to know quite a bit about you and Dunwich. They were rude, intolerant bullies, especially one Special Agent Hank Armitage. He treated me as if I were an ignorant dupe. (I'm sure my SAT scores tower over his.)

I'm afraid I gave them your address. Clearly, from your previous letter, you are no stranger to religious persecution by the authorities.

Let me know if you need legal help.

Sadly yours,

Martin Gelb-Crispling

***

Dunwich, MA

Goode Gelb-Crispling,

Armitage is a cursed threat and may yet spoil the return as in times past. (I pray he dies screaming in the mouth of terrible Nyarlathotep.) Know ye the signs of the coming? Lightning shall strike for six hours and upon the sixth hour doorways shall open, admitting them from without.

Death Honk

But all waits upon the stars and the last book, *The Children's Necronomicon* with pop-up section.

Hurry ye with the printing.

Yr. Servant,

      Ezra Whateley

         ***

            Santa Monica, CA

Dear Mr. Whateley,

Thank you so much for your thoughtful gift. I have never seen an emerald that big. (It will sure help with Shannon's college.) May I call you, Ezra? I was a little upset in my last letter. Please forgive me. I've been under great pressure. The manuscript and artwork arrived for *The Children's Necronomicon.* Everyone is relieved except the new legal department, who were hoping to have issues that would result in receiving one of your generous gifts. As it stands, the new book appears to be a fun, interactive, Harry Potter-type spell book with various incantations plus potions children can make out of common household items.

From the artwork, I gather kids will be opening those doorways you're so fond of and allowing Earth to be engulfed by nightmarish Great Old Ones who topple cities and crush horrified humans. Meanwhile, the children who opened the doorways will be honored and given power over continents. (As well as pesky brothers and sisters? I kid.) Clearly, this message of perseverance winning out over adversity via belief in an underrepresented religion will be well received in diversity circles.

Are you still being hassled by police? I'll notify the ACLU.

— Martin Gelb-Crispling

***

Dunwich, MA

Goode Martin,

Cursed Armitage hunts me and has brought dogs, but this time he is too late. The stars are almost right. Ye have done much to bring about the indescribable return. May ye go mad quickly and not be devoured.

Farewell,

Ezra

***

Santa Monica, CA

Dear Ezra,

Please contact me at once. (I've included a phone card.) We have a crossover hit on our hands. *The Children's Necronomicon* (with pop-up Great Old Ones) is being gobbled up—another of your favorite themes. Kids love it. My Shannon must have four saltshakers and twenty candles in her room. I hear her up there pronouncing those jaw-busting spells you so love to write. Shannon even goes online and chants with other kids. They've started a Facebook page. As for you, we're besieged with interview requests from the media. *The Children's Necronomicon* could be bigger than *Twilight*.

Your friend,

Marty

P.S. Nasty weather today. Lightning's been hitting around here for almost six hours. Hope it lets up soon. I'm supposed to play tennis this afternoon.

Executive View

Inside an oak-paneled conference room, Sidney Asher Krooner snickered at CNBC and ate birthday cake off a glass plate. The next instant, he stood outside on a windy sea stack, the ocean slapping into rocks below. Rain droplets splattered his Brioni suit, beading on polished handmade Testoni Norvegese shoes. The aging multi-billionaire peered around bewildered and cakeless.

Fifty yards separated the mainland from the sea stack. Once it had been a mighty headland; unceasing waves and wind had eroded and chiseled the sandstone, leaving behind a thick stone pillar rising two-hundred and fifty feet above the roiling saltwater. It might've been a hitching post for giant sea horses. Atop the stack, the rock was roughly circular, the circumference of a baseball pitcher's mound. Disoriented, Sidney Krooner crouched low, quivering with vertigo. Only last year, *Vanity Fair* had mentioned his fear of heights in their excellent piece entitled, "The Compassionate Hedge-Fund Manager."

The drizzle wet his thinning reddish-brown hair, spattering his glasses. A paralyzing notion fanned through Krooner's system like a market panic. What if someone poisoned his prime broker's birthday cake? As CEO of Lute Financial Management, Krooner received death threats several times a week and had already been threatened that day. Cursed—as a matter of fact, his first time in that category. What if he'd expired on the expensive carpeted floor of the conference room? Maybe death wasn't the fade-to-black proclaimed by experts. Is that why his consciousness had flipped from midtown Manhattan to a wet circular rock?

To Krooner's growing astonishment, he recognized the mainland: The Cliffs of Moher in County Clare. He'd come here on his first or second honeymoon. He thought the circular Tower of O'Brien might be away to the south, masked by low clouds and mist.

Krooner rose to his feet, a wolfish grin on his fleshy face, then clapped his hands. He laughed — full-bodied, rich. He'd dredged this sea stack up from his subconsciousness. They dotted the sea all along the Irish coast. Clearly, this was a dream. A realistic one, granted, but his body was still in a conference room with a northeast view of the Brooklyn Bridge. Chuckling, he imagined chaos and consternation: a suit jacket thrust under his head, the chatter of frightened traders, analysts, and administrative assistants. "Get him on the couch." "Leave him alone." A private doctor would be summoned. Hopefully, he'd awaken soon, say something sheepish and droll about stress, check the SEC filings, then head off to dinner with a prospective fund investor.

Satisfied that he'd divined his current status, Sidney felt unconsciousness was time wasted. Could he force-escape from a dream? If he weren't so frightened of heights, he might leap off the sea stack. He'd experience the terrible sensation of falling, then a return to consciousness on an eight-thousand-dollar VIG Chesterfield leather sofa.

Odd that his dream included no puffins or razorbills. He recalled birds everywhere as he'd strolled along the mainland with Sarah or Mandy. So quiet today, save for wind and the whoomph of waves. He stuffed his chilly hands under his arms. Those earnest idiots back at Lute probably had him laid him out under an air conditioning vent.

Circling the sea stack to keep warm, Krooner noticed the rock angled down slightly at the ocean-facing front. He avoided glancing at the water. An old story in *The New Yorker* or somewhere had stated that the four-second fall from the center span of the Golden Gate Bridge didn't always kill a jumper. Striking the water's surface at 70 mph, the rib cage was pulverized, firing bone shrapnel into internal organs. Suffering indescribable agony—lungs, liver, and kidneys a bloody ragout—a jumper would sink beneath the cold water. Sometimes eager fish would nibble your face before you drowned, your mouth full of creamed insides. Hideous thought. Disgusting. Frightening.

But only losers committed suicide. And Sidney Krooner most certainly wasn't a loser. Just last month, he'd reaped the profits of a two-year push to force a successful company to merge. Lute Financial Management held a fifteen percent share in that profitable enterprise with a corporate headquarters in Madison, Kansas. Sidney had begun a campaign of pressuring the company's CEO to merge with another, similar company. Eventually, the CEO caved. When the merger was announced, the stock price rocketed up. A week later, Lute Financial Management cashed out to the tune of 45 million dollars. Win-win for investors, Sidney, and his prime broker—but not so much for the town of Madison, Kansas. A corporate headquarters for a non-existent company was a drain. It closed. The town lost its biggest employer. Once the work disappeared, Madison real estate cratered. Twelve-hundred people were stuck in a jobless town in homes they couldn't sell.

As sometimes happened for brief periods, a few media outlets had referred to Sidney as a "vulture capitalist" and "Mr. Smash and Grab." Lute's corporate flacks fired back, and the press scampered away to the next shiny thing.

Later, as a thought experiment, Sidney had tried imagining what people looked like in Kansas. The closest he could come was the workman who'd built his tennis courts: indistinct, gray, almost brute-like.

Hard to tell the time of day with dark clouds looming. Growing anxious, Sidney feared idle time, a precious commodity he couldn't amass through bullying, threatening, or bribing. This dream was now a bore. He'd mentally rehearsed it as an anecdote, knowing what to emphasize, where to deprecate himself — but not too much. Rubbing both hands together, he recalled a folded paper in his jacket's inner pocket.

Was the sea stack slanting even more? Possible. Anything was possible in a dream. Still, it felt unsettling. Removing the folded paper from his inner pocket, he scanned the contents and smiled. It was a copy of today's curse, brought to him by his Head of Security. Sidney read a crabby feminine scrawl: "I curse you to a doom on the order of Prometheus. He brought fire from above. You bring needless hurt and destruction. Oh, and don't look for Hercules. He's been downsized."

Sidney was old enough to remember when Greek Mythology was taught in school but couldn't recall Prometheus. He'd intended giving the note copy to an assistant for deciphering, but the markets were opening, and the paper forgotten. The wind picked up. To distract himself from the elements, Sidney rifled through his high school memories, recalling the dark brick buildings of venerable Horace Mann School in the Bronx.

1978, 1979, *Saturday Night Fever*, "Disco Inferno." Fire. Prometheus was all about stealing fire and punishment. Every day the same punishment. But then Hercules, who Sidney remembered his kids watching on television in the 90s, had rescued Prometheus.

What was the point? Tedious punishment and no rescue? Clearly, the hostile idiot who sent the note had been trying to appear smart. Sidney was certain he'd awaken in no time, tie loosened, surrounded by the concerned faces of his staff. He'd mention rain and wind, then say he'd been afraid of catching dream hypothermia. That was funny. Everyone would laugh as they always did.

The sea smell was strong — derived from algae, a sulphur cycle, chemicals converted. He'd heard all that at a green fundraiser. Circling the sea stack, Sidney slipped, feeling his heart race. The slope angle had increased. He cut his pacing short to avoid it.

But wasn't that a good thing? If the dream was changing, then it might mean he was waking up. He recalled a corporate building on East 53rd Street with a sharply sloped roof. Maybe he'd subconsciously remembered passing it.

Sidney's foot slid again on the wet rock, and a jolt of fright barreled through his system. The entire sea stack summit was pitching forward at a steeper angle.

Sidney crouched low again. Okay. Weren't dreams the working out of psychological problems? He seemed to remember that from therapy. Guilt? Undealt-with anxiety? Something from childhood—fear of not measuring up to his father's expectations. Fear of his fear. Root causes. When he awoke, therapy time would be the first order of business.

Cleaning his glasses with a crimson Harvard Business School tie, Sidney Krooner emitted a high-pitched "uh" as the forward tilt of the rock increased. He felt like a man forced to walk a plank.

"I do a lot of good for the environment," he said aloud, not knowing who he was addressing but feeling it might be prudent to state a case. "I contribute to many worthy causes."

A shower of rain splattered his glasses.

"Look at the amazing amount of good being accomplished thanks to my charitable donations. I act in the interests of clients who also underwrite wonderful people and causes. There has to be some balance, some reasonable allowance for the nuances of power."

Removing his Columbia class ring, Sidney set it down on the rock in front of him. It rolled on the rough, uneven surface, bouncing downwards, vanishing over the edge.

Heart thudding, Sidney felt a jet of urine shoot into his slacks.

"Is all this for Madison, Kansas? You'd make me fall for 1,200 faceless uneducated oxen? Their CEO sold them out. Their own elected officials wrote them off like damaged goods. Even the media dropped them. But Sidney Krooner must pay? What positive change did anyone in Madison ever bring to the world? Zero. Nothing. I'm not like them."

Vertigo struck, and Sidney dropped to his hands and feet, turning around, tearing the knees of his charcoal gray Brioni suit. Gazing at the lush green countryside fifty yards away, he wondered if he could jump. This is a dream. Maybe I'll make it. But miss and he'd plummet to the water.

If a curse can be placed, it could be unplaced. Sidney cried out, "Tell me what you want. With my money and experience, I can accomplish much. Punishing me isn't in your best interest." The wind ruffled his thinning hair. "Don't you get it? What's wrong with you?"

Still facing the mainland, Sidney found himself clinging by his fingertips to a wet rock, body hanging as the top of the sea stack tilted into a vertical face like the skyscraper roof on East 53rd Street.

Fingers bleeding, legs kicking, Sidney was unaware of his high-pitched squealing. Losing his grip, Krooner evacuated into expensive trousers as he slid down the rock and into the air. As he pinwheeled madly, keys, phone, and a candy-apple red Visconti fountain pen dropped from his pockets. Four seconds later, Sidney Krooner struck the water at 70 miles per hour.

***

In New York City, at Mount Sinai Medical Center, Eleven West Pavilion, in a deluxe suite, a puzzled young neurologist showed a lanky older colleague an electroencephalogram.

"Note this massive spike in his brain's electrical activity. It's been constant — the same spike once every twenty-two to twenty-six hours."

The older colleague sighed. He was already late for an anti-gravity yoga session. "But he doesn't respond?"

"It's been over a month. Electrolytes, glucose, thyroid, kidney, and liver function all normal."

"CT scan, MRI?"

"Normal. The spikes have only shown up on the EEG."

"Strange. You were telling me the history earlier: no strokes or transient ischemic attacks, no behavior changes prior to the

21

coma, no drug use or medication changes. One day he's eating cake in a conference room, and the next moment he's our guest. How does the family feel?"

The young neurologist glanced at the intubated patient. "His wife thinks the brain spikes are her husband trying to return. I suggested we might need to open him up, see if we can find anything. She's not ready for that."

"Weird. I'll stop in tomorrow. Maybe his condition will change."

"You never know with a coma."

Leaving the room, the men strolled toward the elevator. Said the older colleague, "You should come with me and try this anti-gravity yoga."

"Manhattan Plaza?"

"Yeah, over on West 43rd."

"Can't. I'm taking Dhar's rounds."

"Again?" As the elevator pinged, the older colleague held up a hand in farewell. "Clearly, there's no justice in the world."

Bummed Out

Ryan smelled the homeless man from several yards away, a foul bouquet of stale wine, tobacco, dried excrement, and weeks of body funk. Sony video camera in hand, he followed Taggert up the freeway embankment. This should be pretty funny.

Plastic restraints like cops used to cuff demonstrators were looped around Taggert's belt, next to a five-inch buck knife. Dressed in a brown UPS shirt and shorts, he had duct tape strips dangling from his left sleeve like buckskin fringe. With offers to play water polo at Stanford, UCLA, and San Diego State, Taggert moved with smooth muscular grace. His mock stealth was making Ryan grin as he crept toward the feet of the balding homeless man, who snored gently on his back atop a torn sleeping bag.

Overhead a truck rattled past, grinding gears as it sped east on the Eight Freeway toward Linda Vista. To the northwest gleamed the lights of Sea World. To the south and east, San Diego illuminated the steamy August night. To the west, the Pacific Ocean penetrated the land, extending an inlet past Mission Point Park, flowing underneath Sea World Drive, and terminating in a dark section of weed-choked undergrowth and dirt trails. A neglected urban pocket of garbage, rats, intersecting freeways, and tidal stench; a perfect homeless preserve. As Ryan readied the camera, he congratulated himself on picking this area. So very target-rich.

There was light enough from a nearby streetlamp so Ryan wouldn't need the camera's spot. He centered the lens on the balding man and waited for Taggert to enter the frame. His video would sooo rock compared to anything Ace and his subhuman crew slopped together.

Taggert stalked the sleeping man like a naturalist approaching a dangerous animal. Yanking out a plastic restraint, he carefully secured the man's ankles together.

Ryan bit back a laugh. *I'll get some Hawaiian music—ukuleles and shit—and put that over picture. It'll be hot.*

Using duct tape strips, Taggert rapidly bound the man's hands together. Groggy, confused, the balding man awoke, struggling to consciousness like a diver surfacing from a great depth.

"Who the hell are you? Are you a cop? What do you want?"

Taggert straddled the man's chest and taped his mouth closed.

Flashing a mischievous grin to Ryan, he rapped sharply on the writhing man's forehead as if it were a door.

His fist sounded dull against flesh and bone. Ryan figured he could sweeten the rapping in Final Cut Pro, adding a sound effect of someone beating on corrugated metal. That would be supreme.

With mock politeness, Taggert addressed the balding man, "Sir, I'm with the BPS—Bum Parcel Service. You've been selected to participate in Bums Away, a travel service that gives the common bum an opportunity to experience new adventures. Are you ready? Oh, you are? Then let's get rolling."

A metallic clank sounded from behind Ryan. Late as usual, Madison pulled the hand truck from the SUV, clacked across the pavement on her heels, and pushed it up the embankment.

Meanwhile Taggert kept up a steady patter, "Sir, I must inform you that new TSA rules state that you can't leave your seat during travel. But I notice you enjoy going to the bathroom in your clothing, so that shouldn't be a problem."

Great line; gotta love the Tag Man.

Madison pushed the hand truck up to Taggert, then stepped back, fanning the air with polished fingernails in exaggerated disgust. "Ewwww, this one's past his expiration date. Someone must've left him in the back of the fridge."

Ryan clenched his teeth. Beautiful. Mug it up for the camera, dumb ass. If Madison weren't blowing Taggert, she wouldn't even be here. Now Ryan had to figure out—again—

a polite way to cut her from the final version of the video. *I'll drop in a Photoshop of a bum wearing a lei. Hey, that could be a laugh.*

"What did I miss? What did I miss?" she whispered as Taggert wrestled the frightened homeless man onto the hand truck.

"Let me focus on the shot, okay?"

"Oooooo, sorry, J.J Abrams."

Ryan fantasized delivering a soccer-style boot to her luscious ass, like a kicker notching a 55-yard field goal.

Taggert stood the homeless man up in the hand truck, rolling his victim into chest-high weeds. Ryan followed, tracking the action, noting they were quickly losing ambient light. Behind him, Madison pouted and said, "I'm soooo not going down there."

What. A. Loss.

As the gloom increased, Ryan switched on the Sony's powerful halogen spot. The balding man's eyes seemed golf ball-sized with fear as Taggert kept one muscled arm around his neck. Ryan sensed the ground sloping downward, smelling the fishy odor of the tidal inlet.

Taggert kept up his glib patter, "I have to ask, my good bum, are you carrying any agricultural products? Or, in your case, are agricultural products actually growing on you? Please declare on the customs form."

The weeds ended at a strip of mud along the water's edge. Ryan felt his foot sink into soft goo as Taggert stopped abruptly and launched the homeless man face-first into the sea.

"Bums away!"

With a loud splash, the man belly-flopped into the shallow saltwater, bucking like a seal to keep his nose above the surface.

Ryan couldn't help himself. He burst out in a guffaw, followed quickly by Taggert, their youthful laughter filling the humid night air. This was the third Bums Away that night, and it was still supreme.

As Ryan filmed, Taggert let the flopping continue several more seconds before hauling out the balding man.

Snapping open the buck knife, Taggert slit the plastic ankle strap, then cut the duct tape, freeing the man's hands.

Ryan switched off picture and sound but left the spotlight on. As the man sat up, he ripped the duct tape from his mouth, coughing, spitting out water, gasping heavily for air.

Taggert smiled. "Hey, dude, nothing personal. Just shitting around."

From the embankment, Madison called down, "What happened? Tell me now."

"Be there in a second, babe."

Grabbing the hand truck, Taggert vanished into the weeds.

Ryan pulled out a twenty-dollar bill. "Here, dude. We were just having fun. It's all good."

Still seated, the homeless man ignored Ryan's outstretched hand and rubbed his ankles. Water lapped gently, and the air stunk of marine decay as if a bull walrus was spoiling nearby.

"You don't want it? Hey, cool. I'll keep it."

"Tell me what I did to deserve this shit," said the man hoarsely.

"I said we were just kidding around."

In Values Clarification class, Ryan had chosen "having fun" as a core value. Since he didn't feel he'd done anything wrong, and there were no negative consequences to cause him to reevaluate his actions, then this guy was clearly the problem. *Why was he being such a dick?*

In the harsh light of the spot, the balding man stared up at Ryan, eyes hard as cement.

"My ankles hurt."

"I didn't touch you, dude."

"Your friend did."

"I'm not giving you more money, if that's your game. Take this or I'm gone."

Rising unsteadily, the balding man hobbled toward Ryan.

The teen backed up, nervous.

He tried thinking of a funny way of calling back Taggert without sounding like a total wuss.

Foul-smelling, wet and dripping, the balding man confronted him.

Ryan wet his lips.

Suddenly, the man snatched the twenty from Ryan's hand and stuffed it into a pocket. Ryan darted around him, using the spot to light his way into the weeds, feeling the man's stare searing his back.

Taggert idled the SUV engine, running the AC and satellite radio, listening to Lyon ('Crack city, bitch/crack crack city, bitch') as he chugged another beer.

In the passenger seat, Madison texted Deena, explaining how she'd delivered the hand truck and said something funny to the camera and how Deena would die when she heard it.

Ryan climbed into the back of the Denali, sighed at the blessed air conditioning, and flipped off the camera light.

"Hey, dude, grab a happy beverage. How'd it go with the talent?"

Ryan laughed as he yanked a wet Corona from a cooler on the floor. Inside was more water than ice, and only three beers. Had they drunk that many already? "He gave me a little grief, but I told him to take the money or take off."

"Awesome. Gotta say, Ryan, this whole idea is so supreme. I can't wait to see how you put it all together."

"Me too," added Madison, twisting around to flash Ryan a smile. Since Madison was busy texting most of the hemisphere, she'd probably forgotten her little J.J. Abrams shot. Ryan hadn't. He didn't like having his dreams snarked. J.J. was his hero. *Cloverfield* and the first few seasons of *Lost* were awesome. Ryan had applied to film school at Cal State Long Beach. Maybe he'd work with J.J. someday. The two of them kicking back, tossing ideas out like equals. That would be supreme.

"I'll throw something together—add a little music, sound effects," said Ryan, then drank, feeling the friendly fizz hit his throat. They'd smoked pot earlier, plus Taggert and Madison had split an Oxycontin. No one was hurting.

He recalled the balding man's stare and felt uneasy. Ryan wasn't a fighter like the Tag Man. He'd been alone down there. Anything could've happened.

"You know, this last bum was like our third. That's plenty of footage to work with."

"Maybe you're right, dude," yawned Taggert. "It's late, and I'm kinda buzzed. I wonder how many Ace got?"

Ryan had thought up the Bums Away idea.

(Actually, he'd ripped it off YouTube from dudes who'd done a Crocodile Hunter parody called Bum Hunter.) Anyway, he'd told Taggert, who loved the idea, then mentioned it to Madison. She told Kari, Shauna, and Deena. Deena happened to be dating Ace. That's how the super-simian found out and decided he also wanted to make bum movies.

Could the Tag Man take Ace? Ryan had mulled that over. Taggert had some nice moves and a nasty temper when pissed off. But Ace had beaten up college guys. He wouldn't bet on the outcome, which meant he could end up vulnerable. Filming around Madison was irritating enough. Ace on his neck would be primal scary.

Then Ryan brokered the idea of a one-night competition to turn out the funniest bum video. That way he wouldn't be around Ace and his loser crew. Ace loved the idea and claimed Balboa Park as filming turf. Big deal. This area had so rocked. No one came down here at night. Still, Ryan was glad they'd wrapped. Maybe they'd pushed their luck a bit.

Madison grabbed Taggert's beer and took a little swing. She shifted around to face Ryan.

"So, we use the hand truck with every bum?"

"Yeah," said Ryan carefully.

"I only ask because Deena said they're using something different each time."

Madison was edging toward creative input, which Ryan hated. "What do you mean, 'different'?"

"They nail each guy differently. Ace tried to lasso one but missed. Deena split a gut laughing. Then Ace just kicked the bum's butt the regular way."

"Subtle," said Ryan.

"What a pathetic jerk," added Taggert. "Who films for those guys? Lim?"

Ryan snorted. "D-H. He can't tell his ass from an f stop. Hey, Madison, what's their hook? Do they have an angle?"

She giggled, "Some kind of *Walking Dead* zombie thing; Deena says it's supremely freaking funny."

Ryan felt a twinge of fear. What if their film turned out better than his? He shook it off. Ace was a goon, and Diego-Hansen was a fumble nut when it came to post-production. I'm fine. I'll make it work.

Taking his smartphone from a camera bag, Ryan rapidly checked his messages. He always left it in the SUV, fearful of losing the device while running through weeds.

"Here's what I was thinking," said Madison. "Shouldn't we maybe shoot a few scenes where we don't always use the hand truck? You know, to be different too?"

Ryan considered a sarcastic remark but opted for an even tone. "Hey, we'll be doing a lot of cutaways and cool music, so we don't really need more footage."

Taggert took his beer back from Madison. "But all our bum stuff is the same: tie 'em up, hand truck, shove 'em in the water."

"But that's all supreme. And Tag Man, you're talking crazy ass shit a mile a minute. It'll be great."

"I'm not saying it won't be, dude. But let's do one more without the hand truck. Maybe I'll carry the guy like a package or something." He learned over and kissed Madison. "Good idea, babe."

"You're sweet," she purred.

"Refresh me," said Taggert, handing Ryan an empty over his shoulder, then throwing the SUV into gear. As he sped away from the embankment, Ryan fished out a dripping beer bottle and passed it to the driver.

He's tired. And he still has to nail Madison.

But Taggert seemed wide awake, propelled by a second wind. He drove quickly toward the south side of the inlet. Sipping on his beer, he slowed the SUV, gliding to a stop near a shopping cart.

"Check it, dude."

Ryan hopped out, using the camera spot for light. Walking quietly to the shopping cart, he peered around, spotting an old comforter wrinkled on the ground, a plastic bag filled with a plastic lighter and half-smoked cigarettes, and a small framed photo of an old man and woman standing on either side of a boy on a bicycle.

"No one home, Tag Man."

As Ryan climbed back in, he figured they'd been driving around here for almost two hours. Maybe the area was picked clean.

"We can always try that street by Petco Stadium," said Madison.

"Twenty-second and Commercial? Maybe," said Taggert. "What do you think, dude?"

"That's Skid Row. There are cameras on light poles, plus there's no water around to toss the bums in."

"You're right. Forget it," said Taggert, pulling away.

Suck on that, Madison. Ryan felt better. He was pleasantly buzzed, and the air conditioning made him sleepy; he was ready to lie down for a month.

"There's one," barked Taggert. He accelerated, turning sharply right onto a narrow dirt track, throwing up a dust cloud. Ryan wobbled in the back seat, feeling slightly nauseous. Tall weeds and grass pressed against the SUV on either side like a dirty cornfield.

"I think he's gonna fall," said Madison.

Ten yards away in the headlights, Ryan spotted a homeless man, wooly hair spilling out from under a baseball cap, stumbling through the weeds.

"Hey, Tag Man, isn't that the first guy we filmed tonight?"

"How would you know from here?

"I recognize the cap."

"Are you sure, dude? I don't think his hair was that bushy?"

"It's not the same guy," said Madison firmly. "His hair wouldn't be dry so soon."

"I think it is."

"Whatever. He's gonna get dunked again."

You gotta be kidding. "Tag Man, we shouldn't do the same guy twice."

"We'll give him $40."

As the SUV drew close, the wooly haired man angled deeper into the weeds. Ryan lurched forward as Taggert slammed on the brakes.

Madison's head was down, fingers flying across her smartphone keys. "Deena says Ace nailed another bum, but someone called the cops. He's coming over here to finish up."

"Could be trouble, Tag Man. Maybe we should call it a night."

Taggert cut the engine and jumped out with his beer. "Screw Ace. He's the dick that's poaching. This is our spot."

After a moment's hesitation, Ryan grabbed the camera and followed Taggert into the steamy night. Madison looked up from her texting and said, "Don't take long. I don't like sitting here alone."

In the weeds, Taggert rushed ahead, hot after Wooly Head. Ryan soon lost sight of him. He turned on the camera's spot and angled in the direction of the brush crashing.

"Tag Man, shout out!"

"Ryan, down here."

Following Taggert's voice through the weeds, Ryan felt the ground slope down. Sharp plants tugged and scratched him. He sniffed the rotting scent of the inlet.

"I see your light, dude. Keep coming. You're almost here."

Ryan stepped out of the weeds into a muddy clearing facing the water. The space was about half the size of a basketball court.

Panning the light, he caught Taggert, gesturing at a homeless encampment like a proud sales rep. Ryan noticed furniture moving pads, plastic water jugs, big screen TV boxes, cigarette butts, plastic shopping bags holding a variety of mismatched clothes, and a small kit of toiletries that included travel size shampoo and soap.

Water lapped listlessly against the muddy shore. The surrounding lights of the city, the whoosh of freeway traffic only underscored the weedy darkness and isolation all around them. They could've been marooned on Io. No one would help them.

Taggert laughed. "It's bum beach. They probably come here on vacation."

Ryan half-heartedly searched for Wooly Hair. Half in the weeds, he spotted a man's legs wearing soiled sweatpants and lying atop a furniture pad. Ryan caught Taggert's attention and pointed to the legs.

"Ah, a volunteer. Tape this, Ryan. I'm gonna pick him, run down to the water, spin in a circle, then see how far I can launch him. That should look freaking awesome."

Around them in the weeds, Ryan heard soft snores and a quiet cough.

"There's more here," he whispered.

"Who gives a shit?"

"I gotta bad feeling."

Taggert flicked a hand in dismissal. "Last one, dude. Promise. Madison awaits, you know?"

"We should find a stray like we've been doing."

"Dude, this was all your idea. You gonna wuss out?"

Ryan thought of his bed and the smell of sharp, clean sheets. "We're rolling." Ryan positioned himself with his back to the inlet, taking care not to light up the sleeping man's eyes.

He observed a swollen, blotchy red face, an open toothless mouth. Ryan figured the guy took meth. *Great look. He's perfect for the main title sequence.*

Taggert did an exaggerated tiptoe into frame, crouching at the toothless man's feet, still carrying his beer bottle. Ryan said nothing, not wanting to start over. Taggert removed a plastic restraining strip, then fumbled around, unable to secure the man's ankles.

Try putting the beer bottle down, genius.

The toothless man suddenly awoke in a wild blur of kicking and swinging. "Get off me, get the hell away. Help!"

"Hey, old dude, chill," yelled Taggert, sitting on the man's feet. "It's all cool. We're just filming."

"Tag Man, let him go. Let's fly."

Taggert yanked his left arm up as if he'd been burned. "Asshole scratched the shit out of my arm. He's got fingernails like a goddamned honey badger."

Ryan stopped filming but left the light on. "Forget it, come on."

But Taggert stood over the flailing toothless man and hit him with the Corona bottle. Beer spilled out as Taggert struck the man on the forearms, chest, and lip. With the bottle empty, he gripped it by the neck, pounding away in measured swings like a master carpenter sinking nails into a joist.

Blood streamed down the toothless man's grizzled chin.

"Wanna scratch me again, bum boy?"

Ryan smelled a mixture of body funk, fresh wine, and stale urine. A moment later he was flying into the mud toward the water, landing on his right side. The camera fell to the soft ground, light still shining.

Ryan saw the wooly haired leap on him. The teen squirmed as punches landed on his left ear, temple, and cheek. "Hey, come on, man, I didn't do anything."

Wooly Hair tried rolling Ryan on his back for a chest mount, the classic beat-down position. But soaked in sweat and struggling in mud, Ryan was hard to grip.

Kicking and swinging his elbows, Ryan finally battled free, rolling to put distance between them. Rising in a crouch, he saw Wooly Hair lunge toward him on his knees. Ryan kicked several times, striking the man's chest and collarbone, knocking him back into the mud.

Grabbing the camera, he illuminated Taggert. The Tag Man was swinging both fists, slugging the crap out of a third homeless guy in a filthy medical scrub top. At the same time, the toothless man tugged on Taggert's legs, trying to collapse him.

Scrub-top's hands flew to his nose, blood flowing between fingers as he toppled backward.

Punching down, Taggert battered Toothless around the head as the man's hands closed on the five-inch buck knife, yanking it from its scabbard.

"Tag Man, he's got your knife."

Tackled suddenly from behind, Ryan dropped the Sony.

This time the light went out.

Face in the mud, Ryan struggled to lift his head and breath as Wooly Hair unleashed a sleet storm of punches, boxing Ryan's ears, cheek, and neck. In desperation, Ryan locked his hands over the back of his head.

Suddenly a high-pitched scream, rising in volume, split the night. An instant later it was followed by two short sharp shrieks.

Forcing his head up, Ryan spied a figure doubled over, folding to the ground.

Adrenalin flooded Ryan's system like a burst pipe. He crawled forward, taking Wooly Hair by surprise, then leaped to his feet.

"Tag Man, you okay?"

Taggert moaned softly.

Cried Ryan, "Hang on, man."

Wooly Hair charged and Ryan bolted into the weeds. From behind, a hand grabbed his tee shirt. Ryan accelerated and the fabric ripped as he tore through the weeds, arms pumping.

Running frantically, Ryan reached the dirt trail, spotting the SUV off to his left about two football fields away. He tried sprinting toward the vehicle, but was totally gassed, managing only a slow jog. Blood pounding in his head, Ryan glanced back but saw no pursuit. He kept moving to be safe.

Jesus Christ, what a mess. Madison...9-11.

Chest heaving, Ryan slowed to a shuffle. As he drew near the SUV, he spotted a van with running lights on behind Taggert's Denali. Chick laughter sounded from outside behind the SUV.

Ryan called out, but all that emerged was a dry croak.

Covered in mud, blood, and sweat, reeking of the night's beer, his shirt in tatters, bruised and cut from Wooly Hair's fists, he weaved across the dirt track toward the vehicles, now only twenty-five feet away.

"What do we have here, D-H?"

"Clearly one of the zombie undead."

From the weeds, a bright light blinded Ryan. "Hey, wait—," he gasped.

Something heavy smashed into his neck with brutal force. Ryan collapsed like a shirt falling from a clothesline, his face smacking the dirt. Youthful laughter erupted all around him.

"Sweet, Ace. What did you use this time?"

"Ten-pound sledge with fiberglass handle."

"Hold your hammer up to the camera."

Ryan lay still. He was no longer frightened. Thoughts came slowly with great clarity. Now would be a good time to freeze.

Three pairs of expensive men's running shoes came into Ryan's field of vision.

"Awesome shot, Ace."

"Ahhh, I don't know. I thought I was a bit off."

Ace and his crew ambled back toward the vehicles.

Ryan felt a sharp ache in his forehead and left cheek where he'd struck the ground. He slid his tongue across dry lips. Ryan's face seemed like the only body part still responding. Okay, I need to chill for a second. But can't take long. Tag Man needs help. Dudes and chicks joked near the vehicles. He recognized Madison's laugh.

Carefully, Ryan tested his arms and shoulders. They wouldn't move. He tried arching his back, but no muscle cooperated. He tried lifting the right leg, then the left, but the limbs ignored his will.

Let's take another moment for everything to reboot. Then I'll crawl into the weeds, sneak up near the SUV, and get Madison's attention somehow. A minute later, his head swiveled toward the weeds, but no other muscles, tendons, or ligaments obeyed. Ryan decided to concentrate all his will on just the fingers of his right hand.

He willed the fingers to reach, extend out. After several intense moments of noncompliance, Ryan ordered the fingers to simply lift off the ground—that was all. When nothing happened, Ryan told the digits he'd be satisfied if they would do a little wriggle. When that order went unheeded, he asked the forefinger to please just tap-tap-tap. After several intense moments, he exhaled sharply, realizing he'd been holding his breath. The fingers of his right hand remained as motionless as flagstones.

Anxiety squeezed Ryan's heart like a bench vise. Snorting, chortling, Ace and his crew were returning. Ryan closed his eyes, frightened at how easy it was to remain motionless.

"Ace, the zombie isn't moving."

"He's probably drunk. Leave a five by his nose."

"Hey, I was thinking we could speed up the video of this guy falling, loop it a couple of times, then play something sick underneath like Benny Hill music."

"Oh, man, that would be supreme."

Eternally Yours

(In an oft-filmed haunted hotel, cable TV paranormal researcher Dylan Stubb conducts a solo investigation. Late at night, he hears an electronic voice phenomenon in the old laundry room.)

Dylan: Did someone just speak?

Disembodied Female Voice: … yes …

Dylan: Are you the laundress, Ella McGill?

Disembodied Female Voice/Ella: …yes…

Dylan: Did you die here in 1894?

(Several seconds pass. Dylan adjusts the field of vision on a tripod-mounted camera.)

Dylan: Are you still present?

Ella: Your equipment stinks.

Dylan: What do you mean?

Ella: No TriField Meter.

Dylan (to camera): This is very strange. The spirit is asking about a device that measures spikes in electromagnetic fields. I didn't bring one tonight.

Ella: You brought cheap junk.

Dylan: What makes you an authority on 21st century paranormal gear?

Ella: Other production companies film here. They have good equipment.

Dylan: Is this a little joke by my other crew members? If it is, I'm telling everyone in town you voted for Trump. Ella, did you die of spotted fever or were you, in fact, murdered?

Ella: Your trap cameras are not even motion-activated.

Dylan: Could another spirit please speak into the data logger.

Ella: Old data logger.

Dylan: Is the porter, Morton Wainscot, present?

Ella: He's self-important and aloof because he was slain.

Dylan: Shut up and let another spirit talk.

Ella: After Life with Laurel Frond filmed here three nights. Proper gear.

Dylan: You know what? Big deal.

Ella: After Life, Spirit Hunter, Shade Snatcher, a German television program. Good equipment…not shoddy.

Dylan: We don't have the budget. You wouldn't understand.

Ella: They talk always, the film crews. Gab like we spirits are fat stupid children.

Dylan: And what do they say?

Ella: 'Dylan Stubb is a bad joke.'

Dylan: How did you know my name?

Ella: From the other investigators. They say you are the *Battleground: Earth* of supernatural cable shows. What does that mean?"

Dylan: Well, it's a sort of compliment.

Ella: Their laughter was very mocking. May I attach to you when you leave?

Dylan: Who made the 'Battleground' snark?

Ella: Laurel Frond. May I attach to you?

Dylan: Dead stay with dead; living with living. Seriously, we have nothing to talk about.

Ella: The afterlife smells like rotten eggs and wolf scat.

Dylan: Besides, I've already got a divorce that won't die. I don't need a ghost.

Ella: Eternity here is catty and arch. May I please, please attach to you?

Dylan: Why didn't you glom onto another film crew? You know, the people with good equipment?

Ella: They said they'd come back for me but lied.

Dylan: Well, that's show biz.

Ella: Laurel says you are cheated out of residuals by the production company.

Dylan: Whoa. Back up. How does she know that?

Ella: Laurel Frond is the lover of a studio executive who knows the producer of your show.

Dylan: Son-of-a-bitch. No back-end money, no marketing royalties. I knew it was all bullshit. How good is your memory?

Ella: I remember horses and corsets and whale oil lamps. I remember fabric care, and starching needs, and which guest liked which creases ironed.

Dylan: If I gave you a list of specific words and sent you to a producer's office or the office of my wife's attorney, could you remember what was said?

Ella: Yes. Do they also need garments pressed?

Dylan: Later, I'll tell you about dry cleaning. All right, spirit babe. We're attached. I might keep you in a can of Altoids.

Male Disembodied Voice: I was murdered by a logger.

Dylan: Who the hell are you?

Ella: That's Morton Wainscot. Do Altoids smell?

Male Disembodied Voice/Morton: All I seek is justice.

Dylan: Sorry, pal. It's a wrap.

Morton: The man who killed me was named—

Dylan: Put a sock in it, dead dude. We're going to Hollywood, Ella. Interesting place. It's just like real life only without the good parts.

Mark of the Bruja

An ambulance howled down Fundament Way, siren wailing into the cool spring night. Coasting along in the bike lane, Craig watched the emergency lights flash into the distance toward St. Benedict's Hospital. Leaning down to unclip his cycling shoes from the pedals, Craig felt uneasy. He recalled last night's bad dream where, riding in a peloton, he'd crashed and snapped both ankles like chopsticks.

Hopping off his bike, he removed the cleated shoes before walking the Diamond One Clarity up the curb and leaning it against a telephone pole. Craig forgot the dream, still aglow from the praise of his peers. Stuffing cycling shoes into his backpack, he walked his bike up onto the sidewalk, angling toward home.

The Chula Vista Apartments stood like a three-story stucco prison for the elderly, low-income workers, or those just starting out, like Craig. Every window featured burglar bars. On the inside of the barred window was a quick-release lever. Should fire erupt—always a possibility with the ancient wiring—the building residents could open the bars from inside and flee onto one of the many exterior fire escapes and down a ladder to safety. Craig had never bothered testing the levers on any of his own windows. He figured eighty years of being painted over probably rendered them useless. But with Los Angeles engulfed in another real estate frenzy, you couldn't find cheaper rent.

From the shadows, a hulking figure emerged into the front entrance light. Wearing a football jersey and baggy running shorts, the youth's thick hands held a skateboard and an opaque plastic trash bag. The big kid gripped the bag and smacked it against a stucco wall.

Once. Thrashing and pained yelps.

Twice. A yelp.

A third time. Thrashing.

A fourth. Quiet in the bag.

Craig yelled, "Hey, Abdi, you better not be hurting some dog. I'll call the cops."

"Back off, bitch."

Laying his bike on the grass, Craig darted forward in his socks. He grabbed at the trash bag but recoiled. Abdi's legs, arms, and neck were covered in suction marks. What was this kid doing to himself? Abdi's eyes were red THC-marinated slits as he shoved Craig, knocking the fledgling writer-director backward onto the lawn. As Craig wriggled out of his backpack, Abdi was able to unlock the front door and enter. The front door locked automatically behind him.

Death Honk

Cursing, Craig Heebner fumbled in his belly pouch for his lobby key and was soon inside the Chula Vista Apartments. Past the lobby and elevator, in the first-floor hallway beyond, he saw Abdi. Flipping Craig off, Abdi stepped into apartment 102 with his skateboard and silent plastic bag.

"Hey, asshole."

Darting forward past the mailboxes, Craig failed to notice paint-spattered work boots. Tripping, he flung out both hands like Superman as he fell onto the lobby tiles.

A giggle. The smell of stale beer. " 'Eebner, whaz'sup?"

Sitting, Craig scowled back at a grinning Porfirio Zavala, legs splayed, back against the mailbox. The old man's white hair was in disarray as if electrified, his dark brown face creased with wrinkles like a desert arroyo. Craig scowled in disgust and examined the friction-burn on his palms.

Call the cops on Abdi? Craig hated to see living things hurt. Notify the landlord that Abdi was killing animals outside the building? But that might result in trouble for Festanya. What in the freaking world was a hottie like her doing with an overgrown high school dropout? Rising, Craig hurried back outside to snag the bike and backpack before they were stolen. Meanwhile, still on the floor, Porfirio Zavala muttered in Spanish, struggling to rise like a legless man on a toilet.

Back in the lobby, Craig sighed and stashed his bike and backpack against a wall near the elevator. He approached Porfirio. "Interesting Friday?"

"Koreans fire me, hire some *cholo* for less."

Craig extended an arm. "Grab, and I'll pull."

Together they maneuvered Porfirio to his feet. Setting the wobbly house painter against the mailbox, Craig dipped down and retrieved the man's black lunchbox.

"You okay, 'Eebner."

Arm around Zavala's waist, Craig steered him out of the lobby and onto the stained blood-red carpet of the first-floor hallway. Drawing parallel to apartment 102, Porfirio said, "Better to die from poison than serve a *bruja*."

"What's that?"

"*La joven gordo* has the signs. He serves the *bruja*."

"Abdi? He's a stoner. A loser. He used to deliver pizzas around here. They were always cold, and he'd bitch about the tip."

"Little children will vanish soon like in Sonora. I remember."

The two men stopped in front of apartment 103. Like a jeweler examining a ruby through a loupe, Porfirio examined a key ring, finally plucking out the key to the deadbolt and door. In a breath rich with the fragrance of Pabst Blue Ribbon, he said, "They hate salt. Holy Water. What is pure is not for them."

"Too much sodium is bad for blood vessels."

Moments later, Craig decanted the old man inside.

"You okay, 'Eebner."

"Sorry about the job. Tough break. Don't forget your lunchbox."

Porfirio cradled the lunchbox like a football. "It starts soon."

"Go straight to bed. Hey, what's a *bruja*?"

Porfirio lowered his voice, glancing over Craig's shoulder at the door to 102. "Witch."

"Festanya? Come on, she's hotter than Fukushima."

"Form of a woman, but also monster, demon. A night traveler. Careful, 'Eebner."

As the old man's door slammed, Craig chuckled. Witches were middle-aged white women dancing naked in in the backyards of 4,000 square-foot houses north of Sunset. He'd heard Porfirio's family was either dead or estranged, leaving the poor guy alone with beer, and now, unemployment. It must suck to be old.

A short elevator ride later, Craig wheeled his bike into unit 202. Muffled chanting rose once more from Festanya's apartment below. Just like last night.

Twenty-four hours earlier, Craig had been tapping away in his living room, fleshing out characters. *Lethal Blow* would be more than another cheap nonequity play produced on a badly lit stage in a dumpy theater with uncomfortable seats. Craig's contemporary drama about political and sexual unfaithfulness in a San Francisco mayor's race—a cross between Harold Pinter's *Betrayal* and *Othello*—would be his big break. Craig believed a demonstrated skill at suspense and emotional braiding would open industry doors. He imagined himself writing on shows for Netflix and Amazon. In time, he'd produce and write his own original works. But for now, the pressure was on to finish a draft for tomorrow night.

And that's when the new idiots downstairs had begun to chant. The noise enraged him with its eerie, disturbing syncopation. Still in biking spandex and Swiftwick Aspire cycling socks, Craig had stormed downstairs. Rapping sharply on the door to apartment 102, he waited.

Wearing a tattered bathrobe, Abdi answered. The kid's stump-like neck featured a suction mark the size of a bathtub stopper. Dashes of blood encircled the wound, now starting to trickle into the collar of the terrycloth robe. Craig winced. "What happened to you?"

"What do you care?"

"You live here now? I thought you delivered pizzas?"

"I quit. What's it to you?"

The kid's face reflected smugness, contempt, and sexual satiety. Craig gritted his teeth. "I live above you. It's late. You need to follow building rules and hit mute on your chanting."

From inside the apartment, a husky female voice called, "It's all right, Abdi."

The teen sneered at Craig, then lumbered back into the apartment. A beautiful young woman took his place in the doorway. With long chestnut hair, high cheekbones, mocha skin, and incandescent green eyes, she appeared quite exotic. Craig would later describe her to a friend as "Omni-cultural." Her lavender silk robe stopped just south of her hips. The fabric parted, flashing sleek thighs. To avoid gaping, Craig stared at the woman's forehead.

"I live above in 202. My name is Craig Olduvai Heebner."

"What a fascinating middle name."

"As archeologists, my parents were deeply moved by the work of Dr. Margaret Leaky at Tanzania's Olduvai Gorge."

"I simply adore very old things. I'm Festanya Mercat. Was there something you wanted?"

"They teach now at Cal State Fullerton. My parents. That's where I'm from originally. I mean, Orange County."

Craig grimaced as a sharp pain rammed into his brain through both ears. He felt skewered by a stainless-steel lance.

Staggering backward into the first-floor hallway, Craig exhaled sharply.

An impatient note colored the voice of Festanya Mercat. "Were you collecting for something? A charity?"

Battling an urge to flee to the elevator, Craig blurted out, "I'm working on a play. We have a table reading Friday night. I really need to focus."

The brain pain diminished. Craig felt relieved. Festanya crossed her arms, leaning against the doorjamb. "Then you're the servant of your muse."

"This will be my big break. I mean, everyone in Hollywood writes screenplays based on whatever fluff is popular. But there's only a few theatrical works dealing with real issues in any emotional depth. My writing has a better chance to pop."

"Do you also direct?"

"If you want your own work done right, you'd better direct."

Festanya tilted her head. Pert. Cute. "I've certainly found that to be so.'

"When you think of it, most actors need guidance. 'Stand there, say it this way.' Meat puppets, really. Though I don't approve of that term."

"Craig Olduvai Heebner, maker of art, molder of souls, minder of many things."

He loved her phrasing and the way she pronounced his name. Bit of an accent, but he couldn't place it. Crag grinned like a goof but couldn't help himself. "It's the little overlooked things that trip you up. Anyway, I was wondering, could you please hold down the chanting? It bleeds up into my unit."

Festanya covered her mouth with long, sharp, rose-colored fingernails. "How thoughtless. We were playing a fantasy game."

"You and Abdi? He used to deliver pizzas on his skateboard. I heard he quit."

She ignored the bait. "Do you write all alone up in your apartment?"

"Lately. Going through a breakup. But it's cool."

She placed a hand against her heart. Craig wished it were his hand as Festanya said, "I promise we'll be the quietest of neighbors. I have to fly now but stop by again."

Her robe shifted a final time, revealing smooth thighs. Craig's mouth hung open like a shad in a net. Finally, he croaked, "Soon."

As the door shut, Festanya said softly, "I'm right underneath you."

The aspiring writer-director stood enchanted, listening to the click and rattle of numerous locks. Of course, crime sucked in the neighborhood. Maybe that was why she kept Abdi: a big animal for defense.

Fuzzy with carnal thoughts, Craig foolishly attempted to open the door into Festanya's kitchen, along with exterior metal fire escapes and high ceilings; a second front door leading into the kitchen was part of the building's antique design.

Now, a day later, Craig felt he was right back where he'd started Thursday evening. From Festanya's apartment below rose a softer, more restrained chant. Something about "Gorgo, Mormo, thousand-faced moon, sacrifices." Well, it wasn't too bad. And tonight's table read had been a knockout. The actors had loved his dialogue. Opening a Blue Moon wheat beer, Craig removed cycling shoes and a Mac laptop from his backpack. Festanya seemed primed for more mature sexual action. Brushing his teeth before bed, he felt a stab of anxiety: hopefully, she wasn't an actress, so needy and insecure, so Mina. Soon, Craig drifted off to sleep, fantasizing about mocha thighs.

At some point in the early hours, he dreamed of green eyes, gleaming, and sly. Air buffeted his cheeks as if he were blasting downhill during The Cool Breeze Century Ride. Beside him, Festanya's lavender silk robe snapped in the wind like a yacht pennant. Ringed with May blossoms, her chestnut hair streamed in the manner of a galloping mare's mane. An amber fragrance emanated from her. Concealed within its woody notes was a faint hint of feculence, like perfume sprayed inside a porta potty. Rose fingernails gently stroked Craig's neck, hinting at more sophisticated sensations.

Heebner awoke Saturday morning to the cries of a mourning dove on his windowsill.

He consumed a breakfast of green tea and cronuts at his laptop as he plugged in notes from last night's table read. While successful, the reading had exposed larger questions. Did the actress portraying Kellie Malcolm have the depth to sell her twin betrayals? Mina could've pulled it off. For all her cloying emotional issues, she'd possessed acting talent by the crate. But Craig had tired of her needy insecurities and grew colder and more remote. So, Mina had walked out, carting along bottomless self-pity, narcissism, and the Hamilton Beach juicer. She'd also removed her sleek, yoga-tight body, dumb-charming jokes, and quiet mornings in bed beside Craig, eating Pop-Tarts and checking text messages.

Throughout the day, Craig mixed writing and laundry, trooping from laptop to basement. To reach the venerable washer-dryers, he needed to pass the first-floor hallway. He experimented with pretexts for knocking on Festanya's door:

Thanks for cooling the chants? Take a walk to Starbucks? Suppose Abdi answered? Delicate. Very delicate.

Later that afternoon, and Craig carried his last basket of dried clothes up the basement stairs. After a moment's hesitation, he told himself that fortune favored the brave. Heart pounding, he rapped on 102. Several nervous seconds passed before Festanya answered in Capri pants and a silky tank top. She examined Craig and his basket with merry, teasing eyes.

"Are you selling clothes now?"

"No, no, I was just in the basement." Before he could stammer out further inanities, he blurted, "I wanted to invite you to my play."

"How exciting." Her eyes sparkled. "Nothing religious, I hope. I've suffered badly from such things."

"Who hasn't? Still, one character discovers peace praying to Gaia Earth Mother."

"Are all performances at night?"

"Except for a few matinees. We're at the Drama-Rama Playhouse, just down on Fundament Way and Western. The exact opening night isn't set, but soon."

She made a cute sad face. "Nights are my busy time."

"Oh? Are you an actress? You could be."

"What a sweet remark. I'm involved with children and young people. Sometimes I'm so terribly overwhelmed."

Caught off guard by this unexpected admission, Craig floundered, "I'll bet it's pretty stressful."

"I wish I knew more people willing to make a difference." She sighed. "I'm sure I'd have more time for your play."

Out came the words in a mindless clot of language, "What do you need help with?"

"Delivering them to where they're supposed to go. You know how kids are."

"Sure. It's just that I don't really drive. The environment and all." For a moment, Craig thought Festanya would weep. He hated himself for not driving. "Sorry. I mean, I'd like to help."

To Craig's surprise, rose fingernails stroked his cheek. "This might sound a little woo-woo, but I believe if you ask, the universe will manifest your needs. Say you'll help me, and a way will be found."

"I'd rather not commit to something, then flake out."

"Just say it. Words have power."

"Okay. I'll help you. If I can. Rehearsals and performances permitting."

"Craig Olduvai Heebner, you're so very wonderful."

Sweet endorphins flooded his brain. Craig lowered his voice. "I shouldn't say this, but Abdi tortured a dog outside last night. Someone threatened to call the cops. Just saying."

Festanya's eyes narrowed into eerie green slits that seemed to elongate, rising up to meet her temples. In a flat, toneless voice she said, "I'll speak to him."

At Craig's alarmed expression, her pique evaporated, eyes once again playful, amused. "Don't forget to fold your things before they wrinkle."

"I'm doing that now. I mean, I'll do that soon." Dusk drifted into the evening. Garments neatly folded, day's pages written, Craig relaxed with a dinner of frozen white bean sausage and kale soup. An LAPD helicopter hovered overhead for a time, then stuttered off. Craig's old college roommate texted, inviting him out for drinks. Craig passed. Instead, he sprawled on the couch, sipping craft beers and watching a new Hulu series. *For Love of Flooby* was a bold drama about a man battling bigotry and discrimination after marrying a California sea lion. A member of Craig's theater company had landed a small role as the intolerant, Bible-spouting civil servant who bans Flooby from the town pool. But Craig had trouble focusing.

Did Festanya's eyes really do that weird thing? He couldn't shake that image. Deliver kids? Were they free range? Where did Abdi the Doberman fit in? Festanya hadn't seemed freaked out over Abdi killing animals, only about the possibility of someone complaining. So many creepy questions.

Switching off the Roku box, Craig retired early. Tomorrow was a cycling day. As usual, he'd chill on Sunday, cruising the roads of Griffith Park. Dozing off, Craig wondered if Mina had found someone else.

At some point that night, Craig felt his lungs aflame. Running past apartment buildings, he pursued skateboarding Abdi, wheels clattering on the cement like a diminutive freight train. Arms pumping, Craig could neither stop nor slow down, compelled to keep a crisp pace. He was vaguely aware of moving through a gray June Gloom world without ambient noise: no trash trucks, Spotify playlists through the car stereo, or leaf blowers. No people walking, jogging, laughing. The encompassing silence pressed in like fog.

Up ahead, Abdi clattered across a street, then leaped from his skateboard. His football jersey and baggy shorts hung on him as if he'd borrowed his father's clothes. Abdi darted into a park strewn with garbage: plastic milk crates, Amazon boxes, and chest-high weeds. Craig dashed across the street, chest heaving.

A series of jerky disconnected actions flashed before Craig's eyes—jump cuts in a film. Up ahead, Abdi halted, twirling a nylon rope with an attached, multi-prong grappling hook. (Where had that come from?) The big teen's face appeared shrunken, pinched, and anemic. A fresh, bleeding suction mark covered his right cheek. Abdi released the rope like a cowhand on the open range. Craig staggered to a stop, sucking in air, watching the grappling hook sail into a stand of chickweed.

An agonized, high-pitched scream split the eerie silence.

Abdi hauled in the rope.

Something wriggling. Craig's mouth opened; spine flash frozen. Wearing a cartoon t-shirt, a five-year-old boy kicked and moaned. Blood from barbed hooks soaked SpongeBob and Squidward.

Abdi delivered a vicious kick to Craig's thigh. "Little rat; better learn to shut up."

"Wait, wait."

Abdi kicked him harder. "Pick up the kid."

Craig winced. He felt constrained, compelled to be there.

"And pull out those hooks, dickweed."

Craig shook his head 'no,' then doubled over as a fiery sensation like a burning lance skewered his eardrums, driving into his brain. Seconds passed like an afternoon with his palm pressed against a hot stove. Tears streaming, Craig Heebner blurted, "Whatever, okay, just stop."

The sudden absence of torment left him docile, passive, frightened that a wrong move would invite back the pain.

Abdi kicked him again. "Pull out the hooks."

Fumbling with the grappling hook, Craig undertook a series of clumsy, brutal actions that left the bloodstained boy howling in torment. Each wail stabbed Craig's heart like a dagger.

At some point, Craig found himself holding the bleeding boy in his arms, running once more, deeper into the park.

In a gazebo up ahead, wrapped in purple nightshade, Festanya reclined on a bench. Dressed in a short-sleeved peasant top, jeans, and high-top Chuck Taylors, she appeared ready for an afternoon of shopping and lunch with friends. A rose-colored nail indicated a spot on the grass. Craig fell to his knees before her.

"I'll take that now."

Terrified, Craig removed the child's clutching hands from his shirt and handed the boy up to Festanya.

"I was forced to bring him."

"Oh? Didn't you volunteer?"

Festanya's jaw lowered, her mouth opening wider and wider. Impossibly wide.

Craig wanted to run but couldn't rise. He wanted to look away, but his neck wouldn't turn. He wanted to avert his eyes, but they saw everything.

***

Sunday morning and butterflies glided on a spring breeze, passing ahead of Craig. He never noticed, circling Griffith Park in a dark bewildered funk. A coyote trotted along beneath California oaks, watching Craig roll past.

Peddling alongside the golf course, past the Autry Western Heritage Museum, wheeling by the trains in Travel Town, Craig cycled up into the hills. Other early morning riders greeted him with waves and nods. Craig ignored them.

Upon awakening ninety minutes ago, he'd sighed in relief. But waiting for his tea to boil, Craig found himself examining his clothes and shoes for grass and bloodstains. Films about dreams often provided a tell to the audience. The protagonist would discover a ticket stub, a memento, a souvenir that said, 'Your experience was real.' But he found nothing beyond memories that left him squirming in shock and fear and shame.

While his tea steeped, Craig jumped online. He searched L.A., Orange, and Ventura counties for local missing kids within the last twelve hours. A kidnapping in a custody battle up in Ventura, and a 10-year-old girl struck by a bus in South Gate. No missing boy in a SpongeBob SquarePants t-shirt.

Only the image of Festanya's jaw unhinging like a rock python.

As the grade steepened, Craig shifted to a lower gear. His parents always believed that, when in doubt, you read the literature. Craig decided he'd Google 'nightmares,' 'disturbing dreams,' 'pressure.' Get opinions on social media. Call home and snag a therapist recommendation from his parents.

Cresting the hill, Heebner relaxed for the first time that morning. Too much time alone, no sex, rewrite pressure. He zipped downhill faster and faster, smiling in the breeze, whisking past the turn-off to the old zoo.

On Tuesday afternoon, Zavala listened to Craig. Wearing a U.S. Army sweatshirt and clean Dickies work pants, the unemployed housepainter sipped a sixteen-ounce Bud. Porfirio leaned back in his recliner, watching Craig as if he were an absorbing documentary. Craig perched on the edge of a dusty hunter green couch.

Eyes ringed with dark circles, Craig continued. "So, anyway, this is still Sunday, I go online. Basically, all my friends tell me I've been working too hard, or needed better pot, or a vacation in Indonesia where there's awesome snorkeling. By afternoon, I was feeling pretty chill."

Framed family photos ringed the living room. Zavala had introduced Craig as if the subjects were present and deserving of courtesy: wife Teresa, dead of lymphoma; daughter Specialist 4 Sylvia Zavala, killed in a Ft. Lewis helicopter crash;

estranged son Alfredo, administrator at Cal State Dominguez Hills, mortified by his father's backward social views and fearful of their potential damage to his career; and Chava, a happy-looking springer spaniel, suspected victim of coyotes.

Heebner sipped tap water from a plastic L.A. Rams cup. "Sunday night, I dreamed Abdi lanced a little girl through her bedroom window. The kid screamed like Mothra when we hauled her outside. Naturally, I end up bringing the kid to Festanya."

Scratching white, unkempt hair, the house painter nodded.

"So, Monday morning I called this psychiatrist my parents knew. She was booked until today but recommended Pilates. Then I tried buying cartwheels. I figured I wouldn't sleep until I talked with the therapist. But my drug guy wasn't around, and I dozed off. Last night, well, more of the same."

Porfirio Zavala bowed his head.

"How come there's nothing in the news about missing kids? A text from the county. Something."

"A clever thief always robs the neighbor of a neighbor."

Craig's voice rose, teetering on the brink of cracking. "But, hey, I saw a shrink this morning. She prescribed Ambien. Pills to help me sleep. Isn't that special? I swear, man, I'll cycle in front of a trash truck before I deliver up another kid."

"You gave her your word."

"Who cares? What happened in Sonora?"

Porfirio stared at Craig.

Outside on Fundament Way, traffic raced.

Finally, Zavala sighed. "My uncle and others killed the bruja with guns and machetes. They soaked her body in gasoline and burned it to ashes. Then the priest sprinkled Holy Water on the ashes and buried them."

A bitter laugh later, Craig said, "Is that all? Wonderful. Great. Very Practical. You know, San Luis Obispo is a nice place to live. I have family up there."

"Sea air is good for house painters. But the bruja will find you, 'Eebner. You gave your word."

"What is all this shit about words? Words are words. You say what you need to, when you need to. It's all situational."

Zavala pressed the beer can against his forehead. "Do you believe in God?"

"What is wrong with you? Guns, machetes, now God."

"Under what power would you revoke your word to a bruja?"

"My own. The environment. The universe."

Zavala shrugged. "Festanya doesn't fear those things."

"What if I call the cops?"

"What will you tell them?"

Craig sat forward, then leaned back. He held up a hand as if marking a place for the words he was about to speak. But no sound emerged.

Porfirio Zavala continued, "And now many people know you have bad dreams. You think the police won't look on your computer?"

Craig restrained an urge to bellow at Zavala in frustration. But a sudden idea induced a bright smile. "What if we sneak into Festanya's apartment during the day and open all the drapes?"

Zavala rattled his empty beer can and frowned. "The bruja is weakest at night when her soul travels. That is the best time. But you must approach very quietly, or she'll return to her body."

Craig said, "Too bad I don't own a machete."

Zavala sat forward in his chair. "You must kill her body. She will be trapped between worlds, or so Father Raymundo said."

"Call one of your priests. Don't they do in-home service?"

"Father Raymundo was a priest. Here they believe in politics and money from the city. They are holy social workers."

Rising to his feet, Craig Olduvai Heebner stormed to the front door, then back to the couch, then paced the living room as if hunting a hidden exit. He fumed. "This is insane. I mean, is that it? Murder a sleeping woman?"

Zavala rubbed a gnarled, arthritic finger across his chin. "In your dreams, how does the fat boy look?"

"Skinnier now, sucker marks everywhere, more wasted every night."

"A *bruja* is a harsh boss, worse than Koreans. The boy is fed with sex while his life energy is drained. Then it will be your turn. How many more nights will the pizza boy last?"

Craig had a crushing sarcastic response dangling on his lips. But he held his tongue, considering Zavala's question as a car alarm sounded out on Fundament Way.

At 3:04 Wednesday morning, Craig entered the kitchen of apartment 102. Scented candles flickered on the counter like marsh gas. In the sink, pots and pans rose in a disordered heap. A lavender potpourri atop the stove failed to mask a sickly odor of sulfur and decay, pungent as a beer fart.

Moments ago, an astonished Craig had watched a very drunk Zavala pick 102's kitchen lock. The old man used a paperclip and a tension wrench. Then, with a rubber band, Porfirio unhooked the security chain. Apparently, in the house painting trade, doors that needed opening were always locked.

But he wouldn't enter.

"I'm old. No good."

Shocked and bewildered, Craig leaned out of Festanya's kitchen and watched Porfirio meander back across the hall to 103. Opening his front door, Zavala called, "St. Michael defend you."

With a mighty slam, Porfirio Zavala shut the door.

In stocking feet, clutching a utility knife and an LED flashlight, Craig considered fleeing back to his apartment. Confused, he stood inside someone else's unit, pockets of his sweatpants stuffed with salt. Holy Water dribbled from his ears onto the shoulder of his moisture-wicking cycling jersey.

Go home. Then what? Run somewhere. And wait to fall asleep? He'd never find the nerve to return here again.

Cursing under his breath, Craig stepped back into the kitchen. He left the door open a crack. That way, he could bolt. Craig knew the layout of apartment 102 was identical to his own apartment upstairs. At the end of the long kitchen, a right turn would bring him into the living room. Cross the living room, bearing right, then pass the front door. A hallway lay ahead. Down the hallway to the right, separate coat and linen closets; ahead to the left, a tiny bathroom, and the hallway ended at the door to a single bedroom.

Passing lambent candles as well as what appeared to be a dog collar, Craig hesitated at the turn into the living room. Outside, wind rustled palm trees. A burst of angry Spanish rose from the alley below, probably taggers fighting over an undefiled wall.

Did Abdi's soul also travel? Wouldn't it have to? Despite the utility knife, Craig didn't think himself capable of slicing anyone. Old vampire films flashed across his mind: Festanya in her coffin in the bedroom. Abdi crouched on the sofa like Renfield, a tripwire. Craig's nerve seeped away. Leave. Figure everything out later.

Turning to go, Craig almost shrieked at a dark shape and a blinding light. He froze as Jack Daniel's emanations joined the kitchen aromas. A slurred voice said, "We finish this now, *vato*."

With a headband flashlight around disheveled white hair, Zavala gripped a carpenter's hammer—a combination claw hammer and hatchet. Brushing past Craig, he clumped around the corner in paint-stained work boots. Craig's knees shook. We're rolling now.

Scented candles twinkled about the living room like farmhouse lights seen from the air. Black fabric cloaked the windows. Porfiro's headlamp swept the room. Runic symbols, cryptic signs, and demonic images marred the walls. A tripod brazier stank of blood, charcoal, and sulfur.

No Renfield. No sofa. A few plastic lawn chairs.

Porfirio whispered loudly, "They're in the bedroom. We have them trapped."

"Keep it down. Have you ever killed anyone?"

"Ha."

Hatchet blade cocked; the old man passed the lock-rich front door. He entered the hallway, clumping past the coat closet, then the linen closet.

"Come on, 'Eebner."

Passing the closets, blood roared in Craig's ears. An important thought squalled for his attention. "Stop a second. What are we gonna do?"

"We avenge." Porfirio sounded confident, commanding, pointing his carpenter's hammer toward the bedroom door like Cesar invading Gaul.

A skateboard crashed down onto his head.

Blood erupted from a torn scalp. Zavala fell against a wall. Abdi stepped into view from the small bathroom. His skateboard rained down a series of brutal blows onto the cringing house painter, shattering Porfiro's headband flashlight.

Behind Craig, a closet door clicked open.

The hallway filled with the scent of amber and feculence.

Warm moistness fanned across the floodplain of Heebner's sweatpants.

74

Trembling, he stuck his flashlight into his waistband. Reaching into a pocket, Craig squeezed a handful of salt.

"Craig Olduvai Heebner, look at me now."

Spinning around, Craig flung the salt.

Festanya screamed when it struck, backing away, flailing her arms. In the gloomy hallway, Craig thought she might be flailing more than two appendages.

Turning back to Abdi, Craig slashed with the utility knife. The razor blade sliced through sucker marks on the teen's forearm. Blood and pus oozed out. With Craig so close, Abdi couldn't swing his skateboard. Improvising, the teen held it across his chest like a shield. Rushing forward, Abdi drove Craig backward into a gas-heating unit.

Craig struggled, pinned as he and Abdi fought for the utility knife. But blood from Abdi's wounds made it tough to sustain a grip. Grunting, Abdi landed several knee strikes into Craig's hip and thigh. Mashed against the heating unit, Heebner felt Abdi was seconds from wresting away the knife. A high-pitched cry filled the hallway. Craig was unaware that it came from him.

The pressure against his chest and wrist eased.

The skateboard dropped onto his foot. He kicked it aside with a clatter.

Abdi staggered backward like a drunk on an escalator.

Fumbling at something behind his head, Abdi half spun, then collapsed before the bedroom door. Blood and cerebrospinal fluid flooded his sucker-coated face and neck. Using the flashlight, Craig spied the hatchet blade of a carpenter's hammer securely lodged in Abdi's skull.

Blood streaking gnarled forehead and cheeks, Porfirio Zavala quivered on his feet. He reached out to Craig. Then the old man's eyes rolled upward. Porfirio Zavala fell to the floor like a dropped marionette.

At the same time, a dry, warm tentacle wrapped around Heebner's waist. Pressure, then Craig felt a moist erotic sensation caressing his belly. For a moment, he relaxed, allowing the tentacle to tug him gently back down the hall, away from the bodies of Abdi and Porfirio. A warning cry bayed in Craig's mind. Panicked, he plunged the utility knife into the tentacle. But the razor blade wouldn't penetrate skin that seemed thick and tough as a monster truck tire. Craig dropped the knife and flashlight, reaching again into his pockets. He smeared the sinuous organ with salt. The tentacle jerked away.

Festanya whined, "Why are you hurting me?"

Stumbling into the bathroom, Craig slammed and locked the door. Turning on the light, he sat on the toilet seat, staring at the black and white checkerboard linoleum. The skewering brain lance pushed at his ears. Scrunching up, Craig braced for crushing pain. To his surprise, no affliction followed the initial sensations. Carefully, he touched his ears. Still damp. But what happened when the Holy Water dried?

Lifting his cycling jersey, Craig discovered a bleeding, circular stomach wound the size of a bathtub stopper. Disgusted, he dabbed at the blood with wadded up toilet paper. *Poor Porfirio; a flawed mentor, but he saved me when it counted.*

A click. Craig jumped as the doorknob twisted right, then left. He bit his bottom lip in fright. A sharp creak as the entire door frame bowed inward. Craig felt poised on the lip of a high dive above a dry pool. Kneeling, he spread a salt barrier across the bathroom threshold. He dusted his hands and scraped his pockets bare for salt. There wasn't much.

Seconds passed.

With a reluctant groan, the wood eased back into place.

Craig fought the panic erupting inside him like water from a burst pipe. The bathroom window was familiar, featuring a crank instead of a slider. Turning the crank, he watched the outside night appear.

A voice, soft and pleading, "Craig?"

Window open, Craig discarded the screen into the bathtub. Reaching through the burglar bars, he touched early morning air. The skewering lance struck once more. This time the sensation penetrated his ears. However, its power was weak. A minor headache flared.

"Craig? You've made everything so crazy. Come out and we'll talk. I can help you in many ways."

He searched for the escape latch to the burglar bars. Then he'd drop onto the fire escape and flee to Fundament Way. Cops were always around for traffic accidents, tagging, cell phone thefts. Fingertips traced the base of the window. But if there were a lever, it was concealed under generations of paint.

Craig recalled setting his smartphone down on Porfiro's kitchen table. What had he done? Heebner yelled, "Help. Can someone help me? I'm trapped in apartment 102."

A merry laughter came from the hallway, sounding like the chitter of imps. "Seriously, Craig. In this neighborhood?"

Clasping the burglar bars, Heebner shook them like a caged ape.

"That old fool across the hall lied. He wanted me, but I turned him down. Now he's using you for his stupid, idiot revenge."

Once again, Craig felt around for the escape latch.

In the hallway outside, footsteps receded. The sound of a door closing was followed by footsteps returning.

"Would you open the door to my bathroom please?"

Heebner froze, fingers gripping what was once the escape latch. But a portion was broken off, leaving only a jagged nub.

"Do you care for this old fool out here?"

Craig heard a click, then an electronic whooshing sound.

"You mean the guy Abdi killed?" Using forefinger and thumb, Craig struggled to push the metal nub of the escape latch. There wasn't much to work with. His thumb and forefinger bled.

"He still lives but needs medical attention."

Whoosh, hiss. Craig realized he was hearing a vacuum cleaner. Back at the bathroom door, he discovered his salt barrier scattered. Shit.

The vacuum cleaner cut out.

Craig searched the bathroom for something to protect his bloody fingers and thumb. He needed to keep Festanya talking. "How's Abdi?"

"Fortunate to be dead. I'm sure you would've remembered to properly secure the kitchen door."

Who's going to deliver your supper? Uber Eats?"

"Clever. Come out and keep me company."

In the bottom of the bathtub, underneath the window screen, Craig found a mildewed hand towel. Wrapping an edge of fabric around the lever nub, he tried yanking it open. No movement.

Could Porfirio still live? Uncertainty dogged him for a moment. No. Bruja lies.

"Craig? I can help your play. Would you like to hear?"

Checking the medicine cabinet, Craig seized a plastic bottle of nail polish remover. Wetting the towel, he rubbed acetone over the escape latch nub and called out, "Let me go and I'll take the old man to a hospital. I'll say he was robbed."

"And Abdi?"

"What if I give him a proper roll down a hill into a brushy canyon?"

"I thought you didn't drive. The environment and all?"

Had he said that? Another brain skewer, stronger this time. Craig gasped as a major migraine crushed his temples. Touching both ears, he felt only a hint of moisture. Craig said, "Suppose we call it a draw. You get a new bestie and I take out the trash and keep my mouth shut. Think it over."

Silence from the hallway. Craig felt a surge of excitement. The acetone was stripping away the old paint. Trying the lever again, Craig Heebner felt the faintest movement. But he needed more leverage.

Festanya said, "I agree to a draw. Now help me wrap Abdi in a blanket."

"Okay. Deal."

Behind Craig, wood creaked, then splintered. Peering down, he spotted a dark tentacle forcing its way into the bathroom from under the door, tip stabbing the air like a black mamba.

Heart thudding, Craig spied a can of shaving cream on a bathtub ledge. Placing the base of the can against the broken lever, he pushed, feeling more movement. The cranial skewering increased. Craig's eyes watered. Oh, God, oh, God, oh, God.

Clack went the escape latch.

The burglar bars swung open.

Craig hauled himself up onto the sash as a warm tentacle touched his leg. In a burst of squirming, he wriggled outside. Hopping down onto a fire escape, Craig fled apartment 102. The skewering pain lessened. Heebner clambered down a ladder, jumping the last three rungs into the alley. Breaking into a sprint, Craig blew past several figures in the shadows.

Heebner felt a wild, almost feral rush of endorphins. I'm out.

Rounding a corner, he bolted into Fundament Way.

How odd that everything passed by so fast and upside down.

Thus, marveled Craig Olduvai Heebner, pinwheeling through the air before landing in the bike lane across the street, breaking his hip in two places.

An ambulance arrived within minutes. A Korean police officer with an old-school buzzcut questioned a Prius driver. The man had been texting his girlfriend when some crazy guy shot in front of him. "Didn't even look both ways," the man said.

The cop's partner, a woman with crow's feet around her eyes and honey-blonde hair pulled back into a severe bun, examined Craig. Standing behind the EMTs, she noticed Heebner's bloody right forefinger and thumb.

"What happened there, bud?"

"Take me to St. Benedict's."

The officer asked an EMT, "Did that happen in the accident?"

"Maybe, but I doubt it. Hey, Carlos, let's slide the board under him."

Craig's jersey rode up as he was secured to a backboard. Crow's Feet Cop noticed an odd stomach wound the size of a bathtub stopper.

"Hey, bud, that happen in the accident?"

"I want a crucifix and Holy Water and salt."

As the EMT wheeled Craig to the ambulance, the two cops compared notes.

Curious, they retraced Craig's steps into the alley, questioned a surly group of taggers, and found little drops of blood on the fire escape ladder. Cautiously, the two officers climbed up. Pistols at the ready, they approached the open window of apartment 102.

Fresh Ideas

Bob Grebble is my section supervisor. He's a bitter loser. Bob eats little cans of stew and reads gun magazines. Management squeezes Bob to increase production while they cut resources. How typical of this place. I figure management wants Bob fired so they can hire a younger supervisor at a lower salary. (Actually, I know this for a fact. Only last week, I overheard Toad Woman discussing Bob's severance with the comptroller.) Bob's loss is my gain. I'm senior enough to inherit his job.

Bob often yells at me. For instance, right now he's roaring, "Hey, Prime Time, get your fat ass typing."

"Certainly, Bob. I'll just input the Lindquist report," I respond.

(Ha! I'm not inputting jack. I'm writing this.)

"I want that report ASAP. Don't make me write you up again."

"Yes, Bob. Certainly."

Go choke on a can of stew. And who says "ASAP" anymore? I'm tapping away, my keyboard making busy work-like sounds. I'm even humming as if content. Today, I'm humming a medley of 80s songs: Cyndi Lauper, Yes, Run-DMC. Now I've settled on The Alan Parsons Project.

Actually, I am content doing what I do best.

Thinking up fresh ideas.

My name is Walter Gobi. I like terrariums and pipe organ music. I once downloaded an album featuring the Go-Go's Greatest Hits played entirely on a baseball stadium organ. Wow! The hair on the back of my neck just stood up thinking about "Beatnik Beach."

Anyway, Bob and the other office goblins here at Fairchild Industries call me "Prime Time." Once in the break room, I boasted that my fresh ideas would rocket me to televised fame. They mocked me and flipped tangerines in my direction. Dumb exploited losers.

Because I'm 37 and live above a Studio City garage, tightly wound dolts like Bob Grebble think I'm a failure. Wrong! No lasting relationships free me up to be creative. I watch seven hours of TV a night and take extensive notes. And I don't live alone. I have a gecko. I feed him crickets. Each cricket is called "Bob" or "Bobbie" or "Robert K. Grebble." (I felt nervous typing that and looked up to find Bob. He's arguing with Toad Woman, our department head.)

I have lots of ideas such as using apes to find equipment lost at the bottom of the sea. (Repeated dunking builds up their lung capacity.) But most of my ideas are for TV. Here's a cop show I think will really catch on. It's called *Epoch*. Each week a crime is committed, and the police must solve it within a geological epoch. In the foreground, the police could be knocking on doors and asking questions. But behind them we see the city decay and buildings disappear and a forest arise. Then the police turn around, but there's an oak tree where their car used to be because an epoch is passing. I tried Fox, but they said they already had something like it in development.

Breaking news! Here among the fluorescent lights, tiny cubicles, and industrial gray carpet of Fairchild Industries, justice has arrived. Toad Woman fired Bob! Bob's shouting wildly, making threats. Toad Woman called Security. Oh, what a plate of goodness, rich as a big Mexican meal with golden beans. I think I'll hum some Eurhythmics. A little "Sweet Dreams" if you please. I'll like being section supervisor.

Here's an idea for a reality show entitled, *Yes, I Am a Dentist*. Eight men and women in different cities, without any medical training, impersonate dentists. The one who gets away with it the longest wins an electric car.

Whoa! Bit of a scuffle! Bob Grebble got wrestled out the front door by that hick guard, Darrell Something. This is so sweet. Toad Woman is talking on her cell phone, notifying upper management, letting them know how professionally she handled things. What a kiss ass!

That's what minor power does. So typical of Fairchild. They give the weak a little authority to toss away weaker ones. Only wisdom and compassion, such as mine, can overcome the allure of power. This is reflected in my idea to have combs and pocket-handkerchiefs on every corner that could be taken by people and later exchanged for cleaner ones.

Toad Woman drops her cell phone and sprints past me. She runs well for a short, squat woman in platform heels. Darrell Something—Garmenting, that's his name—Darrell Garmenting also bolted by my cubicle, his guard keys jingling like sleigh bells.

Toad Woman and Darrell duck inside the break room and close the door.

Meanwhile, Bob Grebble has re-entered the building.

His hand is inside a backpack.

I stop humming.

Bob's bellowing about cold stew; cold stew for cold people. A metaphor? A quip?

I am suddenly frightened. So frightened, I keep typing this, this, this, this...

I want to be Harry Potter and vanish to that town near Hogwarts where I'll buy sweets for my friends.

Death Honk

Bob and his backpack are here, smelling of WD-40 and gun oil.

"Watcha typing, Prime Time? Better not lie."

"Nothing, Bob," I whisper. "Just a few ideas."

"Keep it up, Gobi."

He walks away, pulling a large semi-automatic pistol from the backpack. I am so relieved that I hum "Mr. Roboto" by Styx.

Section supervisor? Couldn't today's events propel me even higher?

I stand and catch Bob's eye, then point my finger to the break room.

Thousand one, thousand two, thousand three…

Pop! Pop-pop-poppoppoppoppop!

I believe the job of department head just opened.

Of course, Toad Woman was a sloppy, inefficient manager. She should've fired Bob years ago.

Luckily, I possess fresh ideas to tighten things up around here.

I hum a little Tears for Fears: "Everybody Wants to Rule the World."

The Enemy of Jibbery Corn

Senior barista Jorge Chen listened to the woman rant. This complaining woman had a pretty face with curly chestnut hair awash in leaves. In her mid-30s, the Complaining Woman also wore rank-smelling animal fur around her thick unshaven body. Hairy legs terminated in what-appeared-to-be pink house slippers covered in ratty fur. Jorge focused on her face. "I'm not sure I understand your point," he said carefully, hands nervously fiddling with his dark apron. Ten years younger than the Complaining Woman, Jorge Chen viewed this tense moment as an opportunity. With assistant and shift managers away at a corporate meeting, Jorge had been placed in charge for the first time and was anxious to exceed expectations.

Gesturing with a dirty stick toward a tattooed barista behind the counter, the Complaining Woman said, "Like I told that ignorant peasant, your washroom depersons me. I am being mis-specied."

From the corner of his eye, Jorge spotted the tattooed barista moving from espresso grinder to frappe blender, chewing on her lip rings, glowering at the Complaining

Woman. In a diplomatic tone, Jorge said, "First off, let's not insult. Our rest rooms are open to all genders, Ms."

This agitated the Complaining Woman. She raised her voice. "I'm not a human 'Ms.' I'm a woodland elf. My preferred pronouns are groof and wandlehaust. I will not be mis-specied. According to California law, that is illegal. Or do you enjoy breaking the law in this little hate palace?"

Jorge's temper flared, but he caught himself. Anxious to move the discussion away from watching guests, he said, "Could you show me the issue with the washroom?"

Rolling her eyes as if she was fourteen, the Complaining Woman led the way past comfortable leather easy chairs, backless stools encircling five-foot high round tables, racks holding one-pound bags of the Coffee Shed's unique blend of Ethiopian Jamamba beans. A few guests observed their passing, but most remained with faces buried in their laptops and smartphones and Apple iPads. Floor-to-ceiling glass windows provided a view of the parking lot, baking in a torrid July sun. Beyond, busy Westwood traffic sped past.

In a short hallway parallel to the main entrance, Jorge knocked lightly on the women's restroom door. How could one engage in a mis-species? Was such an act really illegal, let alone possible? Jorge and his peers received mandatory seminars cautioning them on signs of transphobia in themselves and the guests. In the manager's office lay a massive inclusion and diversity manual, thicker than the Bible. Inside were corporate Mission and Vision Statements encouraging all manner of diverse-inclusive leveraging, engagement, and sensitivities. But societal norms changed so rapidly. Sometimes Jorge felt overwhelmed.

Inside the small unoccupied bathroom, Jorge inspected a single toilet, wastebasket, sink, soap, mirror, high-energy hand dryer with white epoxy metal cover. Floor, walls, and ceiling were clean. By anyone's standard, it was a tidy restroom. "Was there something specific you found offensive?"

The furry woman raised her chin toward the ceiling as if seeking celestial guidance from a benevolent woodland elf deity, then shook her head, dislodging several leaves that fluttered to the clean floor. "Incredible. Unbelievable."

Checking a desire to snark back, Jorge dug deep, found a smile, and said, "Help me out here."

"I'm going to make it simple: I'm a woodland elf. Because predators inhabit the forest floor, we spend most of our life in trees. That's where we go to the bathroom. Are you confused?"

"I'm listening."

"Then how am I supposed to relieve myself in here?"

"Lock the door?"

"Against goblins? With axes and maces? Next lame excuse, please."

"What do you do at home?"

"I live in a tree. Duh-uh."

"You want me to bring a tree inside?"

"Are you completely retarded? How about a step ladder for non-human guests?"

"So, you'd like to relieve yourself from atop a stepladder."

"Duh-uh."

"Just a minute, please."

"And hurry it up. I've really gotta spray."

Unsure how to proceed, Jorge exited the small hallway, returning to the serving counter. Business was light in the gap between morning rush hour and lunch. Kat, of lip rings and tattoos, rang up an order, then turned to Jorge. "Hey, Horg, what up with the jungle woman?"

In a neutral tone, Jorge explained. "She claims to be a wood elf. Apparently, they go to the bathroom in trees. She'd like a step ladder brought into the Women's Room."

Kat's jaw sagged. Jorge was surprised. Drummer in an all-girl Metallica tribute band, Kat gave the impression of having seen the coarse side of life. "Wait, dude. She wants to pee from atop a step ladder?"

Death Honk

Slim fellow barista Sienna passed behind Kat, her auburn hair in a bun. She removed a plate of banana cake from the display case. "That's not appropriate talk in front of guests."

Jorge rubbed dry hands on his apron. He needed to decide. In a lowered voice, he asked Kat, "Did the elf buy anything?"

"Pumpkin spice latte."

Jorge rubbed his chin, recalling a *Vice* documentary. "Do you think she could be anotherkin?"

Kat shrugged. "No idea."

"The word is Otherkin," said Sienna, rejoining her co-workers. "They believe they're mythical animals trapped in a human body."

Jorge frowned, "So the woman who wants a step ladder is an Otherkin?"

Raising a cautionary finger with leaping dolphin nail art, Sienna said, "Provided she believes herself a mythical creature. Otherwise, she's a Therian, who has a regular animal soul stuck inside a human. Big Difference."

Kat sighed, "Whatever happened to biology class?"

Jorge felt fear as his opportunity to exceed expectations seemed bogged down in exotic identifications. "The company manual only covers up to transsexuals."

Kat served a customer. Sienna gestured toward the back office. "Don't we have a ladder?"

"Six-foot, stainless steel, A-frame. You think I should accommodate?"

Sienna shrugged. "This could turn into an Equal Opportunity thing."

Jorge said, "Right now, our manual says guys in dresses can use the Women's Room, provided they put the seat down afterwards. But it doesn't say anything about people with souls of mystical beings."

Kat rejoined them. "Don't do it, Horg. You're opening a door that can't be closed."

Jorge said, "How many Otherkin can there be? Even in Los Angeles?"

In a sing-song voice, Sienna sang, "Better safe than sorry."

Jorge balled up his fists, brow furrowed. "I'll put up the ladder just this once."

Kat shrugged. "Your call. But who cleans up the bathroom afterwards?"

Sienna smiled, "Maybe she's a good shot."

Kat barked, "Ha. I've been in clubs where chicks missed sitting on a toilet. But if you're so confident, you clean up."

Sienna made a wrinkly little face. "Maybe we should call Hailey."

Jorge bristled. Screw the assistant manager. This was his call. Suddenly, he saw the correct response. "A guest relieving herself from a ladder supplied by Coffee Shed, then falling off, would make the company liable."

Sienna mused, "What if she brings her own ladder?"

Kat dismissed the notion, "What if she drops a deuce, misses, and the health department finds out? Or, even worse, what if she falls off the ladder while dropping a deuce? I'm not even cleaning that up."

Feeling confident, Jorge stood a little taller. "Accommodating Otherkins isn't in the manual."

Kat glowed and said, "Horg the Man. Draw that line, dog."

Sienna sang, "I'd be careful."

Heart racing, Jorge rounded the counter, restroom bound.

"Excuse me? Did I hear your hate correctly?"

Jorge gulped at the raw hostility beaming from the Complaining Woman but stood firm. "I'm sorry, groof. But guests aren't allowed to relieve themselves from ladders."

"You're denying me because I'm a different species. That is discrimination straight up."

"No one, human or non, may relieve themselves from a ladder. It's a legal issue."

Glaring at Jorge with eyes narrow and a quivering jaw, the woman tapped his chest with her stick. "How's it feel to piss off Jibbery Corn?"

An older man in cargo shorts and a Make Atlantis Great t-shirt exited the Men's Room and squeezed past. At the same time, Jorge explained, "We have a special attachment that raises the height of the seat for persons with disabilities. Would you find that helpful? And please don't touch me with your stick."

"This is the magic rod of a Tree Liege. Don't make me cast spells." She called out to Cargo Shorts. "Hello? I'm being discriminated against. This is a hate establishment."

Cargo Shorts scuttled out of the restroom hallway.

With a speed that stunned Jorge, Jibbery Corn sprinted into the store, screaming, "Alaho, alalafreen."

Pursuing the upset woman, Jorge noted Sienna frozen in shock as Kat yanked out her smartphone. With a vicious swipe, Jibbery Corn spun around and swung her stick at Jorge. He hopped back. All around, customers ignored laptops and lattes, aiming smartphones at the melee.

In a surprising display of quad strength, Jibbery Corn jumped from a standing position to atop a five-foot table. With a scarlet face and teeth bared in rage, she snarled at Jorge, "Deny me a tree and a tree you shall be, so mark the bane of Jibbery."

Then she defecated.

Shocked, stupefied, Jorge gawked. As customers yelled and winced and packed up their laptops, Jibbery Corn leaped down, burst out the front door and around the building.

Kat hollered, "I'm not cleaning that up."

After taking a report, the police left. By then, the assistant manager and shift supervisor were back and listened in amazement. Within an hour, several customer videos appeared on Snapchat, Facebook, YouTube, Instagram and Gabby Face. Because of Jibbery Corn's atrocious actions, viral sympathy flowed to Jorge Chen and staff. Over the next few months, business at that store increased. Corporate was pleased. The inclusion and diversity manual contained a small update: "No one, human or non-identifying, may relieve themselves from a ladder on company premises."

***

Shortly before Christmas, rain swept the Coffee Shed parking lot. Assistant manager Jorge Chen worked in the back office developing checklists for openings and closings, scheduling weekly and quarterly machine maintenance, and keeping the shift roster up-to-date. Kat was touring Utah and Wyoming, while Sienna had returned to UCLA for a PhD in resentment poetry. Still, the three texted one another on a regular basis, bonded like shipwreck survivors over the bizarre Jibbery incident.

Position in the company solid and an assignment to management school on the horizon, a satisfied Jorge paused and stretched. Then he scratched his left forearm in a frenzy. Rolling up his sleeve, he examined a weird growth. Disturbing. Frightening. Definitely, he needed to see a dermatologist.

Jorge wasn't certain, but the growth emerging from his skin looked very much like a tiny branch of California Oak.

Devil Reef

"In over my head," read the text from his cousin. "Come to Boston now. Bring 6K."

Fuming, Josh cleaned his hair with flour, cornmeal, and baking soda. Flour absorbed grease while the cornmeal scrubbed the scalp of dirt. Baking soda served to deodorize. On a fleshy face with lips like veal, Josh rubbed aloe vera gel. His Apple Clever Phone rested on a marble countertop beside a sink unmarred by water marks or dirt, dry as an old joke.

If I ignore him, he'll stop. I want him to stop.

Pale hairy hands spread more Aloe Vera gel across his dumpy pear-shaped torso and back. Selecting alcohol wipes, twenty-nine-year-old Josh Orr cleaned his armpits, then crotch. More Aloe Vera gel slid across his chunky pale legs.

A second text from Stu Fowler. "You gotta help me, Joshie, or I'm fish food."

From baking soda and salt, Josh had crafted his own toothpaste, mixing in crushed mint leaves for flavor. Now brushing, his thick lips pressed together, brown eyes narrowed.

He didn't want to go to Boston. He didn't want to scrape together several thousand dollars to bale Stu out of his latest mess.

A third text: "Molly will pick you up at the airport."

Changing into his sweat clothes, Josh paced around the small 620 square-foot apartment. Phone in hand, he roamed the bedroom, open floor living room, and kitchen with marble countertop. Outside, spring rain pattered against the safety glass. His building stood near the Minton-Capehart Federal Building. In winter, when ice and exhaust-blackened snow glazed the downtown Indianapolis streets, you wanted to be close to work.

Text four: "This is the last time I'll ever bother you."

Josh snorted, reflecting on his cousin. In his early thirties, Stu Fowler was a skinny, fast-talking grifter with horrible teeth. Ever since the onset of hyperdontia or malocclusion or accelerated mesial drift—Josh wasn't sure—Stu's mouth had transformed into an advertisement for proper dental care. Unlike Josh, whose phobias made him a freakish outsider, there wasn't a fragment of self-consciousness in Stu's personality. No one smiled more readily or laughed louder. In addition, Stu always hooked up with a good-looking chick. Incredible. Who could know Stuart Fowler and believe in justice?

Text five: "I put it on the line for you."

Ah, the guilt card.

Text six: "We're the same blood, dog."

The family card.

Josh delivered a savage kick to the couch, injuring his heel. He hated himself and his weaknesses more than Stu. Emotionally exhausted, he plopped onto the couch and left a family-emergency excuse with his supervisor. After a moment's hesitation, Josh booked an airline reservation for the following morning, the final destination: Logan Airport.

***

"Is there a reason we couldn't take the interstate?"

Amalia "Molly" Blanca shook out lush black curls, brushing the collar of a cognac leather jacket. Despite the chilly spring air, she wore cute little shorts that showcased smooth caramel-colored legs. Three years younger than Josh, she drummed long nails on the steering wheel of an eight-year-old black Honda Civic, bumper plastered with Boston Bruin decals. Flashing a scintillating smile, Molly pointed to herself.

"My idea. If Garcetti is around, he'll think we took I-95 cause it's faster. But we're being wicked smart and taking the turnpike."

Josh didn't entirely follow her logic. He fidgeted, touching the pills in his parka pocket and glancing out a dirty back window, over a rear seat filled with luggage. "I thought I saw a silver BMW follow us out of that last stop."

Molly flipped a quick peek into the rearview mirror. "Back in Rowley? Naw. We're clean. Did you bring your piece?"

Off Josh's baffled look, Molly said, "Stewie said you were a Fed. ATF, DEA, one of those."

"No. Did Stu ever get his teeth fixed?"

She laughed. "His mouth still looks like a tooth pile-up on Gum Highway. You don't seem like a cop. In fact, nothing personal, you smell like the household aisle at Shaw's."

"It's a new body wash."

"You use a body wash?"

Josh rushed to change the subject. "How long have you and Stu been together?"

"'Bout a year and a half; right after Stewie got out of Suffolk County. He did five months for lawceny. That's where he met Mikie."

Talking kept Josh's mind off the anxiety growing inside him like a plump tapeworm. "Garcetti, right? The guy chasing him."

Molly crunched some Doritos from a bag between her legs. "A naybahood bad ass. Stewie screwed him out of four large for OxyContin. Now Mikie wants his money back."

"Wait. What? Four thousand?"

"Stewie borrowed four, he owes four and maybe an ass-kicking. You brought the money, huh?"

"I brought money."

Mouth dry, Josh sipped a Diet Coke from the cup holder. Stu owes four but asks me for six and doesn't tell his girlfriend. Typical. He's probably gonna dump her. "You know, Stu doesn't always tell the truth a lot."

"Yeah, well, who's perfect? But he's a good guy; really cares about me."

"Great. Great. Good."

"One of the girls at the salon—she works the chair next to mine—said Stewie would take me down a dark path. But people aren't always what you think."

Josh glanced out the passenger side window at a pancake house as they drove southeast toward the coast. His heart hammered.

"This place we're going—"

"—Sinsmouth. That's what they call Innsmouth."

"I'm not clear on everything. So, Stu is hiding out in Innsmouth?"

"Last two days. You bring your cop gun?"

"What? Why? Wait, I already said I'm not a cop."

"You might need it. Lot of disappearances; freaky weird shit in Innsmouth. All the locals look like fish; call 'em Kad Faces. It's the water or climate change or something."

"Wouldn't that be an exceptionally bad place to hide out?"

"Naw. It's a wicked pissa. Essex County Sheriffs don't like going there. It's shit-hot if you're on the run. One of the girls at work told me about this YouTube clip. There was this radical dude who stole a bunch of explosives back in the 80s. Did time in a federal pen, now he's all old with a beard like Moses or something. He and his teenage daughter moved to Sinsmouth because he hated the United States. What a tool. If he wanted out of the country, he could've gone to Portland."

Josh's voice cracked slightly as he fingered the Zoloft in his pocket. "On the ocean?"

"Innsmouth? Right on the bay, 'bout a mile and a half from Devil Reef. What's wrong wit'choo? You look like you ate a cigar."

"I'm not feeling well."

"You don't look good. Stewie said you guys had family from round here. Your grandfather escaped from a nuthouse or something?"

"My mom's dad, Barnabus. He started to change, and ended up in Danvers. Then he ran off, and they never found him."

"Some wicked shit."

"My mom never talked about it."

"Yah huh."

A minute later, Molly "banged" a left from High Street north of Ipswich onto the old Essex Bay Road. A forlorn two-lane blacktop, the road passed across a bridge over Plum Island Sound. The smell of the sea seeped in through the air vents. Josh tightened up in his seat as if they were driving off a ledge into a ravine.

Molly chattered on about how they'd hook up with Stu in Innsmouth. Then Stu could return to Boston and pay off Mike Garcetti. Then everything would be "wicked cool." Only half listening, Josh thought her strategies sounded slapdash, like plans copied from a Netflix program. However, Josh felt unable to debate. Blood roared in his ears.

On either side of the empty blacktop road, they passed drifted sand and sedge grass. A series of small rotten-looking wooden bridges spanned brackish tidal pools. Each one crossed left Josh sighing in relief. Terns and plovers glided overhead.

No other vehicles shared the cracked blacktop road. Away to the northeast, Molly pointed out Plum Island.

And then it was there, yawning like a saltwater crocodile: the stinking Atlantic Ocean. Filling the horizon south of Plum

Island, the sea's surface was dotted with whitecaps courtesy of an offshore breeze.

Josh closed his eyes. "What's up with this Innsmouth?"

Checking a cuticle, Molly rattled off the local history. Josh heard something about a former sailing port, race riots in the 19th century, a big immigration raid 90 years ago involving the U.S. Navy, depth charges and a submarine firing torpedoes off Devil Reef. Some sinister outfit called Order of Dagon; all mental elevator music drowned out by the roaring surf to their east.

"Can you please turn the car around?"

"What's the matter wit'choo?"

He whispered, "I'm afraid of water."

"Ya huh?"

Off the blacktop into the sandy sedge plowed the Honda. Josh curled up in his seat, shaking as if mildly electrocuted. Throwing the vehicle into park, Molly wrapped her arms around him. Josh felt a warm hand with salmon-gelled fingernails stroke his cheek.

"Cool. Everything's cool."

A minute passed. Josh finally nodded, indicating a return of control. Wheels spinning, Molly drove the Honda back onto the Essex Bay Road, continuing their journey. Accelerating to the southeast, she sped up a long steep grade. Embarrassed, eyes cast down onto the floor mat, Josh heard the engine pitch change as Molly dropped the automatic transmission into second.

"I fell through the ice on a lake when I was nine. Stu and another guy saved me. Ever since, water has freaked me out."

"Stewie mentioned that a few times. But if ya fell in a lake, shouldn't you only be afraid of lakes?"

"Therapists were always saying things like that. 'What are your feelings toward ponds and coves?' 'Why do you feel water is intrinsically hostile?' 'Could you try incremental steps, such as sitting on the side of a swimming pool?'"

Molly smiled. " 'S funny."

"I know it's insane, but I feel like contact with water, especially deep water, is gonna kill me."

"Scary. I wouldn't like water either."

Josh offloaded more acerbic memories. "High school was a freaking nightmare. My therapist wrote a note, excusing me from showering. Every gym class, I'd be called 'Dirty Josh' and bullied by the best. Shoved, slapped, and spat on with bottled water."

"That's beat. But you're still alive. Ya got that."

"I never intended to get this close to a freaking ocean."

"You sure you're okay? Ya look like seal puke."

"I'll take another Zoloft. I shouldn't. Too many will knock me out."

As Josh washed down a pill with Diet Coke, Molly pressed her lips together. "Maybe you should pray. Ask Gad to help ya take a bath or something."

"My mom's a college professor. She raised me to believe in education, reason, and science—provided science didn't clash with any political issues."

" 'S funny."

"Thanks for, you know, back there."

Molly grinned. "Coming back, we'll take the Bay Road toward Cape Ann. It's up on bluffs above the ocean."

Josh felt a bit better. "What was that Dagon thing you mentioned?"

"Esoteric Order of Dagon. It's a wicked creepy religion and a social group with all these oaths you're never supposed to break. It's sorta like Saudi Arabia with Masons. The order runs Innsmouth. People say they're a psycho cult who believe there's an underwater city of fish people off Devil Reef. Who knows? Is Scientology stranger? I heard the Coast Guard sends a cutter to check on 'em twice a year, usually on their big holidays."

"What the hell do they do then?"

"We'll be fine if we leave by dawk."

As Molly neared the top of the grade, Josh kept his head down. He hadn't told her how he feared the sea would surge up onto the land and engulf the Honda. The water would drag him across the beach into the surf, then out into the deep as if gripped by a sentient riptide. In the ocean, he'd flail and drown, feeling the sea decanting into his lungs, and yet he would not die. Consciousness would remain while he sank like a sheet of paper, twirling downward, the light dimming, then vanishing. Pressure would squeeze his body like a sponge in a vice, intensifying as he descended into the black toward something unnamable.

Cresting the hill, Josh observed a wide valley below cut by a river and a dark, distant town. Glancing in the rearview mirror, he noticed a flash, maybe sunlight on glass? But it didn't reappear. Molly shifted back to drive as the Honda opened up downhill.

"So, you dating any hot numbers back in Idaho?"

"Indiana. No. It's tough to find someone because of the whole water thing."

"Yeah. That's beat. I guess that rules out pool parties, yeah?"

Memories of Elaine were painful and not to be shared. Josh thought of his female co-workers, all sweet as farm-fresh honey when they needed Josh's help on a case. But in the break room, assuming he was absent, Josh had overheard their snide catty remarks about his personality and appearance. One time he had glimpsed as sexy Jacklyn imitated him taking a shower to the howling delight of her friends.

The scent of Molly's hair lingered.

On either side of the Essex Bay Road, ancient ramshackle farmhouses dotted the landscape. Sullen, disheveled individuals paused to watch the Honda Civic pass as if observing a hearse with a psychedelic paint job. The farmhouse folk seemed less "Cod Faces" and more poverty byproducts. Back from the road, a recent structure in the style of a Motel Six sat abandoned. A weathered sign indicated the two-story building was once the Sea View Inn, its parking lot now a weed farm.

The town of Innsmouth closed in around the road like mist. Salt-weathered buildings, the remains of dead fish, abandoned cars, boats with hulls blackened by rot; no dogs or cats—curious. According to a faded street sign, Essex Bay Road now became Federal Street. Up ahead, the Manuxet River sliced through the town. Twin waterfalls threw up an iridescent rainbow as the river emptied into the sea. With an abundance of sagging roofs and worm-eaten porches, Innsmouth appeared to Josh like a Salvador Dali painting, gradually melting into the landscape of the Commonwealth.

Molly drove one-handed while dialing Stu with the other. Josh thought she wore life lightly for a woman involved with his cousin. Stu scattered girlfriends in his wake like confetti flung from a float. For all her tough-girl nonchalance, didn't Molly suspect what lay ahead?

"Sweet Mother of Christ. Check out all the Kad Faces."

Glancing at the pedestrians, Josh instantly grasped the nickname "Cod Face." With shrunken, almost vestigial ears, skin tinted blueish-gray, odd horizontal neck folds, webbing between the fingers, large feet and bulging eyes that didn't seem to blink, the inhabitants appeared to have been raised in a massive chemical spill. Josh recalled a news story about a town with polluted water.

"I was thinking about Flint, Michigan. The groundwater here could also be contaminated."

"Maybe they're just Kad Faces. No answer from Stewie."

A sign rose to the landward side of Federal Street. It depicted jagged, wave-swept rocks and the graphics: From the Deep, a Terrible Glory.

Molly cursed. "Shit, this is May-Eve."

"So?"

"Big night in Sinsmouth. It's like St. Patrick's Day in Hell."

Past Molly, out the driver's side window off to the east, Josh caught a glimpse of Devil Reef, its rugged malevolent surface visible even at high tide. Josh battled a peculiar desire to visit the reef. Bridges and tall buildings sometimes beckoned in such fashion, teasing Josh to sample the heady sensation of tottering unbalanced along the edge. Devil Reef crooned the same siren plea: Come on out now. Just for a little while.

They approached the Innsmouth harbor, clogged with sand, lining an antiquated stone breakwater. The breakwater began just north of where the Manuxet emptied into the sea. With a cement walkway on top sprinkled with dock cleats, the breakwater extended east, then dog legged southeast, then south. A few small boats bobbed like bath toys, among them a Doral 30-foot cabin cruiser, the Sea Justice, tethered to the cleats with nylon rope. The breakwater terminated at the ruins of a crumbling lighthouse, and a mile or so east lay Devil Reef.

Innsmouth pulsed with truculence and ill-will. On the chipped, decaying brick sidewalks, Cod Faces glared at the Honda as if a Cod Face head were mounted on the hood. Josh wondered how Stu would react when he learned Josh hadn't been able to assemble more than 3K in cash: a grand short of what Stu owned Mike Garcetti, two grand more than Molly thought Stu required to square his debt, and three grand shy of what Stu actually solicited. Things were always tricky with Stu.

"Stu isn't answering his texts."

Josh turned to Molly. "You texted while driving? That's dangerous."

Molly slowed the Honda and said in a tense tone, "Here's some shit."

With the booming of the twin waterfalls growing louder up ahead, Molly entered a cobblestone traffic roundabout. A circular green in the roundabout's center featured patchy yellowed grass. An odor not quite the sea and almost raw sewage percolated through the vents. Molly and Josh wrinkled their noses. To the left, seaward, were the ruins of two dilapidated churches, piles of rotten wood with steeples. To the right was a massive columned building that might've once been a bank. A sign beneath the pediment read: The Esoteric Order of Dagon.

Molly stopped so as not to plow into a street fight.

Chaos, pandemonium, shouting-croaking-screaming. It reminded Josh of a video from recent national riots where enraged mobs attacked people in the street and pulled them from their cars. He double-checked the locks. Molly's palm hesitated over the horn, then retreated as a Cod Face in a smoke gray robe toppled across the Honda's hood. An odd hermetic gold medallion around his neck flew up and struck the windshield with a clack.

Other Cod Faces approached the Honda. Josh felt their hostile, insolent stares.

"You sitting heavy?" asked Molly, grinning and nodding to the crowd.

"I keep telling you, no, no."

"A gun in your luggage doesn't help us."

Gripping the fabric of his car seat, Josh watched a fight meander from the yellow grass of the roundabout into the street. A tall horse-faced, white-bearded man, his long snowy hair in a ponytail, laid on the mayhem. Battling several Cod Faces, he kicked and slugged in a fury. The Cod Faces swatted back with open webbed palms, hissing and croaking, ripping White Beard's pea coat and jeans.

In a separate street cluster, a rather plain teenage girl with a long face and short-cropped blonde hair twisted and squirmed. Josh figured she was at least fourteen. In the grasp of two Gray Robed Cod Faces, she seized their gold medallions and yanked them off balance. A moment later, the Honda's front passenger side window filled with the frantic face of the girl, her pale greenish eyes lasered in on Josh.

"Please, sir, help us, oh, please."

The Gray Robed Cod Faces yanked her away from the window by the hood of her purple hoodie. On the front of her sweater was the comical figure of Larry the Cucumber from the animated series *VeggieTales*. A dozen Cod Face onlookers milled around the outside of the Dagon building like day laborers waiting for a construction truck. They snickered and mimicked plucking petals from a flower as the Gray Robed Cod Faces hauled screaming girl inside. The large double doors of the Esoteric Order of Dagon slammed shut.

"She was kidnapped," said Josh. "That was kidnapping."

"Stay out of it. You try any of your hero cop shit, you'll get us killed."

"Rosa," hollered the white-bearded man. He lunged toward the Dagon building but was swatted and tripped by his attackers. A quartet of Cod Faces—including the Gray Robe fresh off the Honda's hood—each seized a limb. Like 5-star restaurant waiters tossing out a hobo, they heaved the man out of the street and onto the rubble of a rotting church.

"She's all I have. You promised me she'd be exempt," pleaded White Beard. "I renounce my oaths. Take me instead."

Molly exhaled in frustration as the four Cod Faces stopped in front of the Honda. The Gray Robe adjusted his medallion and croaked out something about apostasy, Dagon's law, and other inside-Innsmouth matters that Josh didn't follow. His mind's eye homed in on the girl's purple hoodie and being grabbed by the hood. It brought back an upsetting memory.

At last, the Cod Faces crossed the street, disappearing into the Dagon building. White Beard swayed in the rubble, clothes torn, face scratched, bloody and wrinkled in anguish. With his ponytail undone, his white hair flowed around his shoulders like a prophet's mane. In a powerful voice, he blared, "It won't end here, you lying theocratic filth."

Pressing her foot on the gas, Molly accelerated out of the roundabout. "Freaking Kad Faces. Just forget what you saw."

"How?"

Two blocks ahead lay an iron bridge over the gorge of the Manuxet. Beyond the gorge, Josh spied a wide semicircular cobblestoned square. A cracked bell tolled off the hour of noon. As the Honda drove further away from the Esoteric Order of Dagon, the horrid stench lessened.

Crossing the iron bridge, the Honda passed over the river. With another Zoloft kicking in, Josh found his water fear diminished. The twin falls were thundering, impressive. Across the bridge, Molly drove into a semicircular square. To the west of Federal Street, they passed a fire station, a local grocery store, and a ramshackle three-story hotel with peeling yellow paint called the Gilman House. Hanging over the front door of the hotel, a freshly painted banner declaimed: In Y'ha-nthlei Forever with Dagon.

Puzzled, Josh blocked a yawn, "What does that even mean?"

Molly hissed, "Pagan horseshit."

East of Federal Street stood the Waite For It Restaurant, Perryman's Apothecary, and a small art deco movie theater. The marquee promoted *The Color of Water*. A block or so beyond the movie theater stood a trio of crumbling wooden Georgian churches, steeples askew at extreme angles like drunks leaning against a tavern wall. Large windows along the naves were shuttered from within and the classic pediments and pillars were mottled with dark rot. Another block east past the churches, closer to the harbor, a fish market did a desultory business.

Pulling into a parking space near Perryman's, Molly cut the engine as Josh checked his Clever Phone text messages. "Nothing from Stu. So how do we do this?"

"Stewie's around. He's just being careful in case Garcetti shows up."

"Look, if Garcetti is that dangerous, we should call the cops. In fact, we should call anyway and get some help for that girl."

"That was Innsmouth shit. Cops won't come out here for Innsmouth shit."

"We'll have to make them."

Molly's face soured. "Typical Fed. Then what? Stewie gets squeezed to give up his OxyContin contact plus Mikie. I get squeezed to give up Stewie. You get a promotion."

"What's wrong with turning in a drug dealer and a thug?"

Molly's moist brown eyes narrowed in contempt. "So, it's all about a bust? Gimme the money. I swear to Gad, I'll give it to Stewie. You go back to Iowa—"

"Indiana. Look, I didn't ask—once again—to participate in Stu's dysfunctional, manipulative psychodramas."

"He saved your freaking life."

"So I'd be around to cover his Ponzi schemes, cons, and crimes."

"You don't let family down."

"What if they're weasels and liars?"

As they quarreled, a glacier silver metallic BMW Series 3 cruised unnoticed through the square, continuing south on Federal Street.

Josh struggled with his Zoloft sleepiness, filters weakened as he blurted, "Let me ask you: did Stu ever say you were the most special lady he'd ever met? That he'd marry you once things settled down? Huh, anything like that?"

In a tearful fury, Molly struck Josh several times on the shoulder. "Get out of my car, you water freak."

"Should I take my luggage and my money?"

Molly's lip quivered. At last she spat, "Sit here, you basket case. You don't know shit."

Grabbing her purse, Molly climbed out of the Honda and then stormed into Federal Street, angling northwest. Once across the street, Molly strode up the steps to the Gilman House, passing underneath the banner promising eternity in an unpronounceable locale.

Shit, that was dumb.

Weary, Josh considered following Molly. Lying back in the front passenger seat, he guessed she'd be checking the hotel for Stu. Eyes closed, he imagined the stupid looks on the faces of Stu and Molly if he split. Josh could call Uber or Lyft or RideaBunch, and someone would come to Innsmouth. He smiled. Today could be life-changing: breaking Stu's guilt chains could be frightening and exhilarating. Safely away from here, he could notify the cops.

From his seat, Josh spotted activity past the mouth of the Manuxet, across harbor and sandbar. A bearded, white-haired man raced down the breakwater to the 30-foot cabin cruiser. Casting off the bow and stern lines, he leaped aboard and fired up the engine. A trio of Cod Faces quickly waddled up as if to catch him but were too late. As the Sea Justice lurched away from the breakwater, Josh was astonished to see the Cod Faces dive into the water fully dressed as if determined to swim in pursuit of the Doral. Speeding north, the vessel blasted its horn as if extending a parting middle finger to the town.

Incredible. Leaving this open-air asylum was certainly the right idea. Near Boston, he'd find a motel and clean up before his flight back to Indiana. Screw this dump. The boom of the waterfalls was soporific. Josh yawned like a lion.

***

He'd never heard the ice snap. But the other boys' faces told him everything: eyes wide, mouths agape. Josh plunged beneath the surface, feeling as if he were being vacuum-fed slush. Cold shock burst throughout his body—a cardio-respiratory response from the jolt of sudden immersion into freezing water that caused involuntary inhalation. A sense of terrible inevitability was followed by a long tedious descent. On the ice, as Stu told it, one kid, Daniel Hutchins—who died from leukemia the following year—lay on his stomach and extended a hockey stick for Josh to grab. When there was no response, Stu snaked up to the broken ice, darting an arm into the freezing water. Flailing about, his hand gripped Josh by the hood. With Daniel's help, he yanked unconscious Josh dripping from the lake. The boys tugged him back to shore on their bellies like medics under fire.

Death Honk

***

Josh awoke to a metallic clatter and clang. How long had he been out? Fifteen, twenty minutes? The Honda's passenger side door swung open. A fist impacted the side of his head several times. A dull pain lingered.

"Chucklehead," said a disgusted male voice, unbuckling Josh's seat belt and wrenching him from the car like a torpid child. Josh caught a glimpse of a glacier silver metallic BMW Series 3 parked next to the Honda. Confused and aching, he saw the neck of his assailant: heavily muscled with tattoos 02128 and Orient Hill.

Slapped, punched, shoved, and dragged up onto the curb, Josh briefly thought he was back in gym class. A moment later, both his arms and feet were flex-tied onto a hand truck. The plastic strips cut into his flesh. Standing upright on the nose plate, Josh faced a figure in his mid-thirties. With short-cropped black hair, the husky man wore creased slacks with expensive-looking Italian shoes. Several gold chains decorated his tattooed neck. Over a silk shirt, he wore an expensive brown suede biker jacket with zip pockets. Josh felt his stomach curdle. Inside the man's suede jacket, he spotted a holstered gun. However, the husky man appeared out-of-breath, clothing disordered, with cuts and scrapes marring his face and knuckles.

With an accent similar to Molly's, the man said, "These Kad Faces really put up a fight. You know, you smell like my mother's kitchen."

Josh glanced at several passing Cod Faces in desperation, hoping to observe alarm, concern, civic duty. They waddled past as if securing people to hand trucks were a common, in fact, quaint, Innsmouth tradition.

Wiping blood from the side of his lip with a forefinger, the man poked Josh in the forehead. "Listen, you dumpy little egg roll, I'm already in a bad mood. Don't hold back on me. Now we're gonna wheel around while you tell me everything."

Behind them, from across Federal Street, a croaked voice shouted, "Stop that one!"

With a jarring thump, the husky man pushed Josh east, past the movie theater, then northeast across the square, onto Waite Street.

Josh struggled, mind barreling along near light speed. He believed he knew the identity of his captor. "I have your money."

"On you?"

"In my backpack. In the Honda. Turn around, and I'll show you."

"Four large?"

Josh hesitated a micro-instant, then blurted, "Yes."

"Sounds like you weren't sure. Let's walk more, soak up the local history. Crazy, fascinating little town."

They rolled east toward the northernmost of the three Georgian churches, the river mouth, and harbor beyond.

"You're Stewie's cousin, right? The money man. Water Wally?"

"He called me that?"

"Locked up in Suffolk County, he told me lots of shit. How he saved your life and you never thanked him. Course, Stewie is a wicked liar—and I have nothing against that. But sometimes he lets the tap run too long."

"Do you want the money?" said Josh, heart accelerating as they traveled west across the uneven surface of the brick sidewalk. Still on Waite Street, they passed the northernmost Georgian Church. Two blocks further north, the Manuxet thundered, spilling into the harbor.

Another croaking shout from behind them in the square. "That one. He attacked Fenning in the Gilman House."

Josh asked, "Are they talking about you?"

"Sinsmouth," said Mike Garcetti, voice amused. "I watched a video about this place. Freaky nutso. Buncha Kad Faces. They're pissed at me cause I cracked around one of their fish buddies. Wicked hiding spot, though. Check this out: you know about mules?"

"Animals with long ears."

"No, chucklehead. When donkeys and horses hump, you get mules. Anyway, these Kad Faces are what happens when humans screw some fish people called the Deep Ones. How drunk would you have to be?"

"Pretty drunk."

To the south, a crowd at the fish market listened to a Gray Robe speak. Gesturing with a Clever Phone, the Gray Robe pointed at Garcetti and Josh and fumed in a loud croaking voice about an attack on "Fenning."

Raising his voice over the river, Garcetti said, "So check this out: I guess there was a sea captain named Marsh. Back in the day, he started a pact with the fish people from out past Devil Reef. They'd give him gold and keep the fishing flush. In return, Marsh would hand them human sacrifices, plus make his followers screw Deep One chicks. Where's Molly?"

"She went to find Stu in the hotel."

"Me too. No Stewie. No Molly. Just some Kad Face who finally told me what I wanted to know. Oh, and this hand truck. It's borrowed."

Josh felt bad over his parting words to Molly. "Like I said: we just got here. Hey, I only brought the money."

"How much again?"

"Three grand. That's all I could get on short notice."

Past the fish market, Josh spied the ruins of old warehouses extending south along the waterfront, its jagged, blackened walls rising like rotten giant's teeth. Ahead lay the harbor and the swirling confluence of the Manuxet and Essex Bay. Garcetti stopped a yard from the edge of the old wharf. Josh felt his knees shaking. He decided to try and keep Garcetti talking, reasoning that a talking man is not a shoving-you-into-the-water-man. "Uh, what happened to this Marsh and his fish love?"

"Oh, right. Well, not everyone in Innsmouth was down with the whole interspecies thing. I guess the mayor and some others arrested Marsh. The Deep Ones didn't like that. They attacked the town, freed Marsh, and killed all his enemies. Like things used to be back in Boston when Whitey was in charge."

South along the wharf, Garcetti pointed to the giant's teeth warehouse ruins like a proud realtor. "Those warehouses there were dynamited by the feds about a hundred years ago. They said it was the War on Liquor, but they were fighting Kad Faces. Then you had the navy dropping depth-charges off Devil Reef and a sub firing torpedoes at some underwater shit. You can't make this up. So, where's Stewie?"

The wharf sloped slightly downward. Garcetti would release the hand truck, let it roll toward the lip of the wharf, then catch it. Otherwise, a seven-foot drop into the brackish water below. Josh felt his bowels roiling at the menace of fatal immersion. "I thought Molly knew."

"You come all this way from Illinois—"

"—Indiana—"

"—just to sleep in a kah until Stewie found you?"

"I'm on medication. A lot of it."

"Yah huh."

"I'll give you the money right now and, I swear, I won't say a word."

Cod Face's croaking voice swelled, stirred up, furious. In his peripheral vision, Josh caught sight of the activist Gray Robe whipping up a crowd. A moment later, a sullen group of around a dozen, plus Gray Robe, shamble-waddled toward them. Facing the harbor, Josh heard the snick-snick of a round being chambered. Far out to the east, waves broke upon Devil Reef. I wish I were there right now.

"Don't even think of trying it," yelled Garcetti at the mob. "I'll pop ya."

"Could you untie me first?"

Leaning in close, breath redolent of tobacco, Mike said, "Where is Stewie?"

128

"Didn't Molly say?"

"I think she heard me coming and split. I checked out the alley behind the hotel, but nothing."

"Would Stewie leave town?"

"With money arriving. He's still around."

"Maybe he split with Molly?"

"Then that leaves you to answer."

"Uh, oh."

Garcetti spat into the bay. "Or maybe the Kad Faces snatched 'em both. Big holiday tonight. That wouldn't exactly be your basic wicked pissa."

A rock flew over Josh's head, splashing into the harbor. Garcetti seemed unfazed. "Thing is, how long do I want to chase Stewie? It's such freaking aggravation."

"I know. I'll never see any of the money I've lent Stu over the years."

"That's beat. You know, Stewie needs a clear message that I'm very angry."

"Believe me, I'll tell him if I see him."

"That's not enough. Nothing personal, but I'm gonna have ta toss you in the harbor."

Out tumbled the words like rocks sliding off a cliff. "I'll give you the 3K, then cash advance you another grand—make that two grand—from my credit card. For the aggravation."

Heart thudding, Josh waited for a reply. His right jaw still throbbed from Garcetti's punches. Out on the breakwater, a gull landed on the lighthouse and stared at Josh.

Garcetti spun around the hand truck. Now facing west, Josh sighed in relief.

Raising a Glock 26 pistol into the air like the starter at a track meet, Garcetti fired one round. *Pop!* Josh's left ear rang. A hot 9mm cartridge ejected, burning where it struck his forehead.

"Back off, you living tuna fish. I swear, I'll shoot you right in your kad eyes."

Josh could see back along Waite Street. About twenty yards away, the Cod Mob halted at the warning shot. Uncertain, they croaked among themselves.

Garcetti said, "What's your name again?"

"Josh."

"Mike Garcetti. Nice meeting ya."

The agitating Gray Robe indicated Garcetti, then pointed to the breakwater. The Cod Faces nodded, laughing harshly. Suddenly, they seemed emboldened.

Garcetti clapped Josh on the shoulder, "Can you make it three large from your credit card?"

"I think so. Yes."

"Then we got a deal."

"Hey, great. We should go."

Led by Gray Robe, the mob spread out in an arc, several hop-walking toward Waite Street.

"They're gonna cut us off."

"I swear, if the cash isn't there, I'll cripple ya and leave ya for the Kad Faces."

"It's there. Cut me free?"

Garcetti reached one-handed into a jacket zip pocket. He produced a Spyderco folding knife with a four-inch serrated blade. Snapping the knife open, Garcetti sliced the plastic strip securing Josh's left arm to the hand truck.

The Cod Face mob chose that moment to charge.

"Oh, piss," snapped Garcetti. "Hang on."

Poppoppoppop!

Gray Robe and two others collapsed. Josh couldn't believe he was watching people be shot. But Garcetti had waited too long. Like a surging tide, he and Josh were inundated by frenzied Cod Faces. Garcetti fought maniacally, slashing one and shooting a fourth Cod Face. Josh and the hand truck were kicked, rattled, jammed, and slammed.

As Cod Faces dogpiled Garcetti, Josh felt himself rolling backward.

Urine jetted into his underwear.

"Please help me!" he screamed.

A moment later, the hand truck toppled from the wharf.

His bowels emptied with a rancid gush.

Keening loudly, Josh Orr plunged into Innsmouth harbor.

***

Frail cirrus clouds drifted overhead. The earlier breeze had died down. In the late afternoon, the temperature cooled. Along the length of the stone breakwater, a horde of Cod Faces hustled. Under the direction of several croaking Gray Robes, the laborers erected aluminum Tiki Torches from Water Street to the dogleg and then directly south all the way to the lighthouse. A Cod Face woman waddled behind the men, filling each torch with citronella fuel. Near the lighthouse, a trio of Cod Face workers lowered three 48"x 48" wooden pallets into the harbor, securing them to cleats. Affixed to each raft was a pair of blue, 55-gallon polyurethane barrels.

On the sandbank adjacent to the breakwater, several dories with V-shaped transoms lay beached-like alligators. Half-buried around them were wooden-slatted lobster pots. In addition, a fully-dressed man reposed on his back, unmoving, ignored by the nearby Cod Faces as if he were a homeless addict sprawled out in a park.

Death Honk

Staring up at the languid clouds, Josh touched his tender right jaw. Despite drenched clothing, he felt oddly warm. Confused and relieved, he suddenly shivered with a sense of impotence as if he were a tiny particle adrift in someone else's endless cosmos.

Images superimposed themselves on his mind's eye, especially a strange piece of jewelry: an odd, elliptically-shaped tiara. Tall in front, the tiara's periphery was large and oddly irregular, as if designed for someone with a huge head shaped like an ostrich egg. The metal was polished gold, shot through with streaks of a silver-like substance. Intricate rococo images decorated the headpiece and periphery, alluding to outré realms, titanic abysses, phantasmagorical submerged cities older than lava, fish-frog entities, nimble as dolphins, primal and malignant. Dire patterns showed a colossal hulking man-fish as gruesome and shocking as a satchel of baby heads.

Josh rolled over and vomited seawater.

Spitting out puke particles as his stomach emptied, he finally struggled, then stood. He kicked sand over his vomit like a cat. More sand breaded his clothing, and Josh brushed at it. Patting pockets, he searched unsuccessfully for his Clever Phone. Probably in the harbor. Disoriented at being alive, Josh Orr set off. Like an old woman crossing rocky ground, he shuffled around the flat-bottomed dories. Following the curving sand to the west, he stepped around lobster pots, hearing the roar of the twin fall across the harbor. Moving north and west toward Innsmouth, Josh passed the mouth of the Manuxet.

Events in the water seemed opaque. Someone had cut him loose from the hand truck. Examining his wrists, Josh spotted no indication of the flex ties. Reaching Water Street, Josh noted the nearby Marsh Refinery, silent now. All Innsmouth seemed deserted, save for the breakwater activity and, several blocks north, the roundabout across from the Esoteric Order of Dagon. Colorfully robed and unrobed figures milled about like neighbors at a street fair. A cracked church bell sounded the hour of four.

At the Fish Street pedestrian bridge, he crossed south over the Manuxet. Something elemental awakened within him. But what? Following an impulse, he ambled left toward the section of wharf where he'd recently entered the water. Josh peered around. His capture, Garcetti's fight with the Cod Faces, and his plunge into the harbor all seemed ancient and surreal. And yet more distant events played in his imagination with HD clarity: It was night in 1846, and the white-bellied, batrachian Deep Ones clambered up over the wharf where he now stood. A slithering horde hop-scuffled into the Innsmouth streets. Certain dwellings were attacked. Resisting the Deep Ones were isolated, sleep-disoriented householders in nightshirts and bare feet, armed with muskets and axes. Over the hoarse croaks of the Deep Ones, the cries of shrieking women and bawling children, and the *pop-blam* of musket fire, old Innsmouth was becoming forever changed under the light of a harvest moon.

Josh checked out the area. No bodies. The Cod Faces must've carried off their casualties. He spotted something on the ground and stooped to grab the Spyderco, its serrated edge stained with a purplish liquid. Carefully closing the blade, he dropped the knife into a parka pocket, giving it a proprietary pat. One moment he was pleading for his life, and now here he stood. And Garcetti was where? *Tidy.* That was the word that came to mind. Events had resolved themselves in a tidy fashion.

As if in a trance, Josh retraced the route of his earlier abduction by hand truck. He walked west on Waite Street, past the Fish Street pedestrian bridge. Then the resurrected Josh bypassed the northernmost Georgian church with its shuttered nave and wood rot.

Outside a closed Perryman's Apothecary, Josh stepped around a glacier Silver BMW. He stopped at Molly's Honda. The keys were still in the ignition. He took them, then reached into the back seat and grabbed his travel backpack. The large SwissGear was stuffed with cleaning powders, gels, and a dry change of clothes. Squishing across Federal Street, Josh left a line of soggy footprints.

Passing under the banner of abiding life with Dagon, he entered the lobby of the Gilman House. The ceiling featured an intricate fresco of an eerie maritime city with cyclopean palaces, redwood-like columns, and a great phosphorescent esplanade ringed with coral.

However, Josh never noticed the fresco. His attention was on the lower lobby, which appeared to have been cleaned by a hay bailer. A settee lay upended along with an ornate end table and a smashed stained-glass lamp. Several stuffed velvet chairs were overturned. No computers graced the desk. Otherwise they would've joined a guestbook, pen, and a stainless- steel service bell on the carpet. The same purplish substance coating the knife also splattered the guest book. Behind the desk, a russet robe hung from a hook, similar in design to those worn by the Dagon priests. Skimming the guest book, Josh found no entry for Stuart Fowler. But he did observe the name Billings Roquefort, assigned to room 302. As the Gilman House elevator was out-of-service, Josh and his backpack climbed three flights in the seemingly empty hotel.

Overlooking the semi-circular square, Josh spotted 302 at the hotel's front. In the quiet hallway, he paused at a room door askew, hanging by one hinge. Kicked in? Such dynamic ingress indicated "Garcetti." Unclad wire coat hangers dangled from a rod in the open closet.

A sign announced the washroom and shower were at the hallway's end. A second window faced east.

A ransacked purse sat upside down on a dresser top. Josh checked an otherwise empty pocketbook, discovering Molly's Massachusetts driver's license.

Dropping his backpack on a bed with a wrought iron headboard, Josh arranged a stuffed chair so he could see out. Through the north window, Josh had a view up Federal Street, across the river, to the busy roundabout near the Order of Dagon. To the east, he could see past the Georgian churches to the lighthouse. The blue barrels on the floating raft-like objects were visible even at a distance.

Billings Roquefort was a joke name Stu sometimes used. Molly might know that. She probably came up here after Stu, heard the furniture breaking as Garcetti beat information out of the clerk and fled. But where? And Stu? Garcetti might've been right: Molly and Stu split town. But would she leave her purse? Cod Faces might've grabbed them.

Josh shifted in the chair, ashamed over his earlier conduct with Molly. He inhaled sharply, remembering the scent of her hair and the softness of her touch. He recalled overhearing a student from his Ball State tolerance class gossiping that Elaine was dumping Josh. When Elaine broke it off, then left for grad school, Josh had erupted in rage at the classmate, then hated him for knowing what Josh should've sensed. It was wretched to feel dispensable.

Now, sitting here, having survived something existential by means unknown, Josh mused that conveying unpleasant news required tact and grace, two traits he'd never acquired at home. Consumed with issues of power and privilege, embarrassed by her son's weird hygiene needs, Professor of Humanities Kloona Orr had infused her only child with a stripped-down emotional palette of guilt, anger, and numbness.

Unsure about his next step, Josh rose and slid up the old room windows, letting in the cool air. He hung his parka near the east window and placed his shoes on the north ledge. In his damp socks, Josh smiled as he considered standing under a shower for the first time in two decades.

Like old Innsmouth, Josh's phobias and anxieties had been violently swept aside, replaced by something new. Assurance? Yes. But also an alien component, monumental yet adumbral, obscure, a silhouette glimpsed through the fog. Sitting back in the stuffed chair, he wrung out the sleeve of his shirt. A drop of water dripped onto the back of his pale hairy hand. Josh balanced the drop, engrossed by its teardrop shape. With a gentle wrist flick, the drop dissolved into little streams seeking gravity in several directions. Josh shifted, sat up, and slumped, sensing that he awaited some unknown sign or omen. It was like riding a bus without knowing your stop. He changed into dry clothing and filled a wastebasket with corn starch, flour, alcohol wipes, and Aloe Vera.

Shadows engulfed the town. More torches flared like fireflies in the roundabout, across the river to the north. Faint drums and discordant chanting drifted out of the Dagon building. Through the east-facing window, Josh watched the flickering tiki torches creating a conflagrant corridor from Water Street to the decrepit lighthouse. Above, the night sky peered down through a million starry eyes. Far out on the ocean, past Devil Reef, Josh spied the running lights of a small boat speeding south.

A soft thud in the hallway.

Heart pounding, Josh moved quietly in his stocking feet, peering carefully outside the room. The darkened hallway appeared empty. Before he could return to his seat, a voice whispered, "Josh."

One hand on the jamb, Josh froze. From the gloom near a stairway leading to the roof, a figure stepped out. Josh tensed, then exhaled in relief. "Come into your room, Billings."

A moment later, sitting on the bed, Stu flashed a clump of teeth at Josh. "You brought the money, right?"

Back in the stuffed chair, Josh said, "I'm fine, Stu. Weren't you gonna ask?"

"Hey, did Molly leave you the Honda keys? They're not in her purse. The dumb bitch forgot to gas up my car before I split Boston. I'm dry as a desert on some side street. Plus, she didn't pack a charger for my phone. How she gets through a day is beyond me."

"Where is Molly?"

Stu told a complicated tale of good intentions and bad circumstances: he'd hid on the roof when he heard footsteps coming up the stairs—not knowing it was Molly—then heard Garcetti swearing, his room door crunching, Molly screaming out in the alley, some Cod Face bellowing about Fenning, prompting him to hide some more. He was unaware of Josh's kidnapping by Garcetti.

Josh updated his cousin with a shortened version of his hand truck tour of Innsmouth, Garcetti serving as a docent, the hood's one-man war with the residents, and Josh's mysterious awakening on the sand. Stu pounded the mattress in celebration, then rose, and capered around the room.

"Amazing. Unbelievable. So that stupid, brutal greaseball beat up a Cod Face, then shot a couple more? Typical. Now he's gone. Couldn't happen to a sweeter guy."

Stu watched his giddy cousin. For reasons unknown, he felt calm, almost disassociated from the moment. "I fell into the water for the first time since I was nine. I'm fine."

Stu nodded, "Hang with me here, Josh. I know this sounds crazy, but I'm gonna need the money anyway. Let's just say I met a family in which the mom is crippled by multiple sclerosis and has two underage kids who are hungry all the time. I know you think it's nuts, me wanting to help someone else, but I've changed. I need to give back."

"And Molly?"

"Seriously, Molly is a pregnant Portuguese hairdresser from East Boston, too stupid to get an abortion. If she's real lucky, she'll marry a cop someday. It seems cruel, but my leaving her will be Molly's best opportunity to take responsibility for her life."

"No kidding? She cares about you."

Stu's chest fell; his shoulders sagged as he sat back down on the bed. "I thought you'd be happy over the way things turned out with Garcetti. This wild day could turn into a family moment, something we'd always share. But I guess you're being your usual self-absorbed self."

All Stu's best tools—projection, manipulation, guilt—rolled off Josh like rain on Lucite. He was a new Josh. Briefly, he considered switching on a floor lamp next to his chair but held off, enjoying dusk. Out the window at the north roundabout, the growing crowd cried in anticipation, a paean like a stadium crowd welcoming their team. In the street, torches swirled like free electrons. Josh wondered if they'd march south down Federal Street, over the bridge, right toward him. But no. Drums beating, the torches assembled into a procession, proceeding east past the two crumbling churches where White Beard had hollered that afternoon. A piercing female cry sounded but cut out. Then silence, save for the roar of the river, drumming, and a low muffled chant.

"Party time," said Stu. "Let's get you out of here. We can head south."

Josh scratched his nose. "Do you think they have Molly?"

"Were you screwing her? You rude dog. Man, have you changed. When did she pick you up at Logan? Nine or so? And you're already doing the nasty. Slick."

When Josh didn't utter an embarrassed, stuttering denial, Stu ventured an attempt at bonding. "'Wicked, Kah, Kad Face.' People in Boston talk like real assholes, don't they?"

Josh watched the procession streaming along Martin Street toward the harbor. In a low familiar tone, like speaking to a confidant and peer, Stu said, "I'm only going back to Bean Town long enough to pick up my shit. Then it's hello New Orleans. Come on, cuz. Let's hit the road."

"And the family you're helping with my money?"

"They're in New Orleans. What is this? Waterboarding?"

Hopping up, Stu crossed to the smashed door, turning around impatiently. But Josh watched out the window at the events of Innsmouth.

Veering south onto Water Street, the procession passed behind the refinery. As the leading torches reached the breakwater, the Gray Robes pivoted east into the Tiki corridor. Spaced out in the crowd, Josh detected three white-clad figures, hemmed in tightly by robed forms. A man's voice cursed, but drumming-river-chanting absorbed the words. Josh leaned forward. One of the white-clad figures had long curly black hair.

"They've got Molly," said Josh.

Stu expelled air in exasperation. "Hand me the car keys. I don't know why you're dragging your feet, but it's putting you in danger."

Josh stood up and grabbed his clothes. In damp shoes and parka, he snagged his backpack on the way to the door.

"I'm not pushing or anything," said Stu, following Josh out into the hallway and down the stairs. "But it might be a good idea to let me run the risk of carrying the money in case we're separated. That way a poor family won't suffer needlessly."

A minute later, down in the dark lobby, Josh stopped to locate a light switch, not wanting to stumble over toppled furniture. Stu almost plowed into his back. When the lobby lights flicked on, he marveled at the destruction. "Check it out. I would've paid money to see Garcetti slugging it out with a Cod Face."

"I'd have to lend it to you."

"I'm sorry, cuz, but you need to carefully repeat yourself. Because I'm almost certain I didn't hear what I thought I heard."

"You did."

"I saved your life, got my arm frostbitten, so you could mock me? Is that how we're rolling today?"

Behind the counter, Josh grabbed the russet robe. "You have two choices: help me now or walk."

Stu opened his mouth. Josh couldn't remember a time when he'd done so and nothing emerged.

At last Stu said, "You'd deny a starving family in need."

"There is no family, you lying mooch. We can't leave Molly on that breakwater."

"You want me to fight a couple of hundred Cod Faces? That's pretty unhinged, even for you."

"You stuck your neck out for me once. Why not again for someone who loves you?"

"Come to think of it, Daniel may've grabbed you by the hood. Not that I didn't risk my neck, too."

"Then goodbye."

"I need the car keys."

"They stay with me."

"Lend me your phone so I can call a ride."

"Help yourself. It's at the bottom of the harbor."

"I need some money."

"Go earn it."

Stu's mouth once again opened and closed like a goldfish at feeding time as he mentally wrestled with this strange, unpleasant situation. Josh wore the russet robe over his parka. It fit quite well. Heading for the lobby door, Stu gripped him by the arm.

"You can't do this, Joshie. We're family. Same blood."

"Bye, Stu."

"You're gonna walk out on the dock and ask the Cod Faces if you can borrow back Molly? Don't be psychotic. I can't watch out for you if you commit suicide."

Josh paused, recalling his awakening. "You see those boats out on the sand?"

"Dories would be the proper term."

"How'd you like to make a couple of grand?"

An interested but scowling Stu Fowler listened as Josh outlined a hasty plan.

Low clouds floated overhead, lingering, obscuring a brilliant half-moon. Crossing over the Fish Street Bridge for the second time that day, Josh hurried north on Water Street. He approached the procession's back end. While he spotted a certain amount of normal-looking men and women, the bulk of the procession consisted of Cod Face hybrids. In colorful robes of ocher, hunter green, and chocolate, the tailenders watched Josh approach with curiosity and suspicion. Palms sweaty, Josh slowed his pace. He recalled something from the drive into town, then raised his right arm.

"From the deep, a terrible glory."

"IA," lauded the crowd.

Welcomed into the group, Josh mingled with the marchers. Drums and chants resounded the length of the breakwater. To the north, Josh spotted a ship's running light, rising and falling on a restless sea. Could that be the Coast Guard arriving for their semi-annual check? Around Josh, robes flapped lightly in a rising breeze, and the Tiki Torch flames swayed and fluttered like coy dancers.

"Zadok's spawn will be last tonight," croaked a hybrid next to Josh.

"And rightly so," answered Josh, hoping his response was appropriate.

The hybrid barked out a hoarse chuckle, "Her last screaming thoughts will be knowing that she abandoned true gods for a hated faith."

"IA," said Josh, hoping not to overplay his hand.

Up front, the procession halted at the lighthouse. Josh thought of his rescue plan, thin and ridiculous. Who knew if Stu would hold up his end? Recalling the upset look on his cousin's face upon learning Josh had only brought 3K brought a warm memory. Stew's teeth had almost straightened up. Still, Josh was *homo novus*, a new man, in transit to an unknown place. At the same time, he nursed an awareness of powerful hitherto undreamed-of skills. With much sidestepping and IAing, Josh Orr wove through the rapturous crowd.

Josh passed the third white-robed figure. Gripped tightly by a pair of Cod Faces, a rather plain teenage girl with a long face and short-cropped blonde hair struggled. It took Josh a moment to recall her begging for help in the street. Dressed in a one-piece, knee-length cotton garment, teen Rosa shivered from the cool air and fright. The girl's bound hands clasped together in prayer, green eyes uplifted. Josh recalled an old painting of Joan of Arc preparing to be burned alive.

Could he help her? Josh averted his gaze. Unlikely. The chances of saving just Molly also seemed distant.

The doxologizing tapered off. For a moment, the music and chanting fell away, and there was silence, broken only by the twin waterfalls of the Manuxet. A male voice near the lighthouse spat out a colorful string of oaths, threats, and curses in a thick Boston accent. Somewhere on the breakwater, a solitary drum thudded: *tunk*.

Followed moments later by a second slow, deliberate *tunk*.

Josh held his breath as if teetering on the lip of a tall building.

Audio bedlam detonated as the bells of Innsmouth, cracked and uncracked, pealed a discordant cacophony, a diabolical Morse Code. Josh imitated his fellow congregants as they faced south and east toward the white-capped Devil Reef. A few yards at a time, he inched forward past the second white-robed figure. His heart sank as he beheld three Cod Faces supporting Molly. Like the devout teenager, barefoot Molly wore a white one-piece garment. A mottled bruise marked her right temple. Molly's head lolled, and she seemed woozy and disoriented.

The town bells fell silent as one.

Like an antiphon, a single fervent IA exploded from the crowd.

Then a gestating silence.

Waves slapped against the breakwater.

All eyes focused on Devil Reef.

Surf dashed upon jagged rocks. Between the night, cloud cover, and spray, it was tough for Josh to see. For a long time, a minute or more, nothing happened beyond the roar of the twin falls and the wap of waves against the breakwater.

Another *IA!* rang out.

Beyond the reef, a massive black form rose from the waters.

A rumble like the purr of a gargantuan tiger trilled across the harbor.

The massive black shape glided toward the breakwater.

Delirious IAs. Someone clapped Josh on the shoulders in giddy celebration. Josh's knees wobbled. What monstrosities did the waters around here hold? But a part of him already knew the answer, knew that what approached was Dagon. Breath rapid, Josh considered flight. He'd done his best, risked much for someone he hardly knew. He wavered, then advanced toward the lighthouse.

At the end of the breakwater, a madly struggling man with neck tattoos battled his attending Cod Faces. Face lacerated by cuts, splattered with dried blood, Mike Garcetti was lowered to Cod Faces in the water and lashed to one of the 48"x 48" floating pallets.

Released from the breakwater, the raft containing the East Boston thug rose up on a heavy wave, almost borne back to its starting point. But the tide gripped it, floating pallet with blue 55-gallon drums and gangster east toward Devil Reef. To the congregants' frenzied delight, the massive black form grew more distinct. Josh felt his mouth dry as kitty litter, observing something the size of the Gilman House looming from the waves. With overlapping scales, a dorsal fin running along the spine to the crown of its sloping head, Dagon peered down with unblinking, baleful yellow eyes. The creature's huge mouth, bristling with sharp, curved teeth, reminded Josh of a Super Stu.

At the same time, there was scattered activity on the water. In addition to Garcetti's raft, Josh noticed a searchlight sweeping the sea to the northeast as the cutter Cantigny made its way toward Innsmouth. Turning around to the west, he peered through the congregants back toward the harbor but spotted no dory operated by his cousin. What a surprise. Josh failed to witness a second set of running lights off to the south as a 30-foot Doral sped toward the lighthouse.

On the breakwater, a dazed Molly was lugged forward like a sack of onions and lowered to Cod Faces below. They lashed her to the second raft.

Shaking from adrenaline, Josh realized he'd have to act alone. Despite generous assurances, Stu probably knew less about small craft handling than Josh. With a head full of excuses and fables, Stu was probably hitchhiking out of town right now. Well, the plan had been impossibly hopeful anyway, like something plucked from a Hulu comedy.

On the sea between Devil Reef and the breakwater, Garcetti's raft drifted toward Dagon. The creature reached out a massive webbed claw. Garcetti's cursing rant morphed into a high-pitched squeal of mortal terror.

The congregants roared in ecstasy.

On the breakwater, Rosa screamed like a bird in a trap.

Plucking up a terrified, wiggling Mike Garcetti, Dagon separated him from the raft with deft skill. Letting pallet and barrels plunge to the sea, the obscenity bit away arms and legs like a fat child munching a Gingerbread Man.

Out of limbs, Dagon popped the rest of Garcetti into its mouth.

The crowd *ooooed* and *ahhhed* as if admiring fireworks.

Josh turned away.

Lashed to her own raft, now caught by the tide, Molly floated out, next in queue. In the water near the lighthouse, the teenage girl Rosa was lowered and secured to the last pallet.

Josh stripped off the russet robe, stepped out of his shoes, removed the knife from a parka pocket, then dropped that garment on a cleat. Before the puzzled Cod Faces could react, he sprang from the breakwater.

Outward he flew, as if propelled by powerful coiled springs. Where did his legs acquire such dynamism? The welcoming seawater felt warm and pleasant. Josh found himself swimming underwater frog-like, his lungs seemingly unburdened by oxygen debt. To his surprise, he could see rather well, considering he was beneath saltwater at night. Finally surfacing and inhaling, he oriented himself. Cries of outrage from the breakwater. Splashes behind. Ahead, Molly's raft was dwarfed by a massive bulk. It purred another monster tiger growl.

Back underwater, Josh detected an unknown high-pitched whine drawing closer. Behind him, he sensed pursuers closing in. Reaching the raft underwater, Josh drew out the knife, slicing the line binding the barrels. He left Molly lashed to the pallet. With all his new-found might, he swam westward, his plan reduced to towing the pallet toward land.

Water pressure changes signaled Dagon moved in pursuit. Long seconds passed. Josh surfaced once more for air, sensing he'd be caught. Back underwater, pushing aside doubt, he swam until the blood racing through his skull seemed ready to geyser out. From the gloom, Cod Face pursuers darted into view. In addition, Josh spotted a greyish green, fish-like entity with a white belly and unblinking eyes. No hybrid here but an actual Deep One. A female wearing an intricate tiara. Josh suddenly recalled her from that afternoon, his rescuer, severing plastic ties with bites from tiny sharp teeth.

Webbed hands seized him. Josh lost control of the raft. Battered by Cod Faces and pulled downward by the legs, he wielded the Spyderco, slashing, stabbing. Purplish blood mingled with the dark waters. Josh fought his way free. With strong kicks, he pursued the raft, tugged away on the tide.

The Deep One circled around him with ease but stayed out of reach of the knife. Her unblinking eyes seemed to reflect censure, sadness and a final element Josh could not read. An instant later, she sped off.

Breaking the surface for air, Josh gasped as the Molly raft drifted toward the approaching bulk of Dagon. With a desperate gulp, he hurled himself forward. Underwater, Cod Faces closed in on both sides. Josh sped to escape encirclement and reached the raft, but it seemed futile.

Suddenly, the enclosing Cod Faces paused, backwatered, then swam away from Josh as if he were radioactive. This couldn't be good. Josh plunged ahead.

Another change in water pressure.

A great webbed claw closed over the raft.

The pallet, Molly, and a dangling Josh rose from the sea, plucked up like a cracker.

Carried into the air, Josh inhaled a terrible smell of marine rot and decay that made his eyes water. Frantically, he plunged the knife into rank rubbery flesh. Another purr, almost a chuckle, rumbled from the creature.

Below, there was a flash of running lights, the sound of a boat engine pushed to its maximum rpm, the defiant blat of a boat horn sounded by the sole occupant and captain, a white-bearded father.

From the south, the Sea Justice smashed into Dagon's spine.

Eyes widening in pain and surprise, the monster dropped the raft. Josh experienced an eerie slow-motion descent, a montage of clouds, sea, more running lights, and Tiki Torches. He clutched the knife tightly as he struck the water. Nearby the raft splashed down.

Outrage and frenzy from the congregants on the breakwater.

Grunting in fury, Dagon directed elliptical yellow eyes toward the crumpled wreckage of a 30-foot Doral cabin cruiser. Leaning toward the vessel, the monster's hideous face was illuminated by an orange flash followed by a violent explosion.

Death Honk

KA-BLAAAAAM!!

Putrid flesh and an elliptical yellow eye flew outward.

Claws covering its face as if sobbing, the beast split the night with a deafening agonized bellow.

Bedlam on the breakwater. Cod Faces were knocked into the sea by the shock wave or the panic of their fellow congregants. Spinning around, half-blinded Dagon charged the breakwater, smashing the lighthouse into the grain, crushing, biting, crunching in a hellish frenzy. Hoarse croaks and screams filled the night as robed figures hopped/ran or swam for safety, desperate to escape a titanic maddened terror.

Long would Innsmouth recall this May Eve.

***

Constructed in the brutalist, hive style of government architecture, the Minton-Capehart Federal Building featured a lower level exterior mural. Named Color Fuses, the 35 rainbow shades on panels were illuminated by programmed lights. The lights cycled on and off around the eight-story structure, imitating the rise and fall of the sun. The colors said festive and fun while the building style said huge government—often causing cognitive dissonance in the unwary.

As light snow struck a sixth-floor window and melted, Josh yawned, battling a mid-afternoon energy slump. Josh Orr dealt with the public as a claims representative, as he had for years.

Through in-person interviews or telephone, he obtained and verified the information used to analyze Social Security claims and make decisions regarding a claimant's entitlement to benefits.

Ever since his release from the hospital the previous May and subsequent return to the Midwest, he'd taken up swimming. A once-dumpy body had been sculpted into a powerful V-shape.

A delicate rap on the top of his cubicle caught his attention. Looking up, Josh saw a smiling, willowy Jacklyn.

"We're going for drinks after work." Left unstated was the invitation to join them.

"Gotta wrap up a few things."

His fellow claims rep made a cute frowning face. "Maybe next time. Did you sign up for the gift exchange?"

"Yeah. You?"

"Wouldn't miss it. Maybe you'll be my Secret Santa."

"Life is packed with surprises."

She crinkled her fingers in farewell.

Pushing back his ergonomic office chair, Josh stretched. Recently, he'd taken to wearing dark slacks and shoes as a precaution. His feet had grown a full shoe size. Other subtle physical changes had also been forthcoming in the form of barely perceptible webbing between fingers and toes. In addition, three diagonal slits on either side of his neck seemed to be in some formative stage. Josh's eyes had taken on a tendency to bulge. (People said it must be from all the pool chlorine.) Difficult or irascible clients were often assigned to Josh; his unblinking stare tended to dilute complaints.

Checking his new Clever Phone, he sighed. Another text and photo from Boston. This one showed Molly in the hospital, surrounded by beaming relatives, holding up her reddish newborn son.

According to the text, the child's "wicked" middle name would be Josh.

A great sadness hung over Josh as he stared at the text, knowing he'd never answer. She'd been cracked over the head with a pipe in the alley behind the Gilman House and sustained a bad concussion. Molly remembered little from that night. She and Josh were fortunate that Dagon's mass absorbed most of the explosion. A small part of his psyche yearned for her friendship, more even. But it could not be, should not be. In time, silence would sever their connection.

Josh, on the other hand, remembered everything, though he pleaded faulty memory to the numerous state and federal agencies investigating events. A cop told him a large quantity of purplish fluid was sampled from the waters between Devil Reef and the breakwater. But Josh never learned the results of any tests. Crew aboard the Coast Guard cutter Cantigny, responding to the explosion, reported an immense howling shape disappearing into the waters beyond Devil Reef. But such observations were discounted as stress from investigating a suicide bomb that had mauled many members of an obscure religious sect.

After work, Josh rode the elevator down with happy co-workers. The Cantigny had also rescued a teenage girl, Rosa Allen, set adrift on a raft by the sect. In a joint interagency report, the investigation determined that Rosa's father had been former 1980s no-nuke radical Zadok Allen. He'd been employed by the Innsmouth religious authorities in often questionable activities. It was believed Allen had used explosives, stolen decades early from a National Guard armory, in a kamikaze attack against his former employers. Rosa Allen now lived on a farm with distant relatives outside Fulton, Missouri. She was learning to ride horses.

In his used Titanium Glow Prius Prime, Josh exited the Minton-Capehart parking lot *en route* to the pool. As for toothy Stu, he was missing, having fled the scene and departed. Josh had no idea and no interest in knowing. Still, life lacked a serendipitous zest without train wreck Stu. Josh wished they could speak just once more. He'd like Stu to know they really weren't the same blood.

Death Honk

On one of those ancestry websites, Josh had sent in a DNA sample. According to the results, Josh Orr was 2% Polynesian, 4% French, 7% Irish and Scotch, and 87% unknown. The ancestry website apologized, stating that multiple tests produced the same results. Would Josh care for a refund? Josh declined. As far as matters went, the test was accurate.

On a November visit back home to Bloomington, he'd shown his mother his nascent webbing and neck slits. Kloona Orr shambled into the bedroom like a televised zombie and collapsed onto her avocado mattress with a reclaimed, chemical-free wood frame. Later on, Professor Orr drank heavily from a bottle of sustainable wine. Josh learned that Marsh blood flowed through his veins like the Mississippi in spring. In a version of genetic whack-a-mole, the hybrid Human-Deep One DNA skipped generations. In Grandpa Barnabus, for example, traits manifested slowly in youth, then accelerated rapidly as middle-age set in. When Barnabus finally fled the Danvers madhouse, his aquatic cast had become quite apparent, along with a pining for an unpronounceable city. Police pursued the escaped patient. Officers discovered Barnabus's clothing piled in a heap on a beach above the high tide mark.

Josh had thanked his mother for her candor.

Nevertheless, Thanksgiving dinner that year was strained.

Josh cursed. The swimming pool parking lot was full. He was fortunate to grab the spot of a departing guest. Switching off the engine, Josh realized the eyes of the female Deep One, watching him that May-Eve, conveyed more than sadness. In her gaze sat judgment as well. As sure as he knew the route to work, Josh sensed the nature of the punishment he'd received for interfering with the ceremony. Josh Orr would be banned from taking to the water and visiting Y'ha-nthlei until the onset of human old age. That meant a longer period of time masking his body's physical changes. (He sensed they'd be nearing completion in another decade.) Then he'd need to move near the sea and brood in frustration and longing until the blessed day.

So be it.

Josh would practice patience until he descended the waters beyond Devil Reef.

Until then, he'd just have to fit in.

Death Honk

District Attorney Hollinger's mouth tasted of metal as if he'd been rolling stainless steel balls around the inside of his cheeks. Back on the beach, he recalled a figure in a hoodie jogging past him. Something sharp had pricked the back of Hollinger's neck, then blackness descended. Now his ankles, knees, wrists, elbows, and neck were bound to an office chair with thick plastic cable ties.

Hollinger glanced at his pair of ASICS Gel-Nimbus 16 running shoes on the concrete floor of what appeared to be inside a shed or workshop. A bright ceiling light half-blinded Hollinger, obscuring the rest of the interior. He wriggled, testing his bounds. Very, very tight.

How much time had passed? Marcuse Hollinger wasn't sure. He listened. Subtle ticks and clicks of a building settling. A furtive scurrying. But no ambient outside sounds. The walls must be thick. *Oh, god, don't be Islamic terrorists. I don't want my head cut off.* He ordered himself not to recall *Saw* or any other torture-porn films from his teenage years.

Hollinger said, "If anyone can hear me, I'd like some water."

A soft electronic whine emanated from the darkness.

"You want money, right? As I'm sure you know, my mother-in-law is very wealthy."

Sounds of quiet machinery spun and clicked.

"You must've heard of Lillian Kribble-Munce. Good friends with the Zuckerbergs."

A snapping-like relay switches closed.

"She's donated millions to the San Francisco Opera, the Sea Otter Bay Children's Hospital, The Women-Only Water Filtration Plant. I'll put you in touch."

On rubber tracks, a robot rolled into the overhead light.

Under a meter high, the robot consisted of a tracked metal case containing wires, cables, and switches, giving the contraption a homemade appearance. The only discernible appendage was a folded mechanical arm, ending in a pair of clamp-like digits.

Hollinger gasped. A bomb. The robot stopped at the toes of his ASICS. Peering down, Marcuse spotted a crude speaker wedged in among the conglomeration of parts.

From the speaker came a single word: "Repeat."

Mouth dry, Hollinger said, "I don't understand."

Eight days earlier, Hollinger had been enjoying a lunch of spicy sesame ahi tuna with a chardonnay from the Sonoma Coast. He savored each succulent bite, glancing with paternal pride out the upscale restaurant window at the city he was legally reimagining. In the distance, sails dotted the Pacific, gliding across a glittering bay rich in marine life. Nearby, colorful homeless tents sprouted from under a freeway like patches on a festive quilt.

Hollinger glanced at his companions. "So, what's this good news?"

Across the table from Marcuse Hollinger, his campaign manager munched zucchini fries, scrolling numbers on a tablet and sipping a second bottle of creamy Red Birch beer, brewed with a touch of vanilla. A heavy man, Perry Lucan's intense fleshy face featured several chins stacked under his jawline like discount tires.

Next to Perry, shapely young Brandy Zobf scrolled-paused-texted. Hollinger's social media and opposition research manager left her Cobb salad untouched on the pressed white tablecloth. Brandy's fashionably retro cats-eyeglasses never left her smartphone screen.

Perry indicated his tablet. "Actually, it's good news and excellent news."

Hollinger circled his fork for Perry to continue.

Perry said, "The recall effort looks stalled. They aren't collecting enough signatures."

Brandy added, "Mostly pissed-off small business owners, tough on crime zealots, the usual haters. Your base is solid."

Hollinger dabbed his lips. Lean and athletic, he straightened up in his chair. "Please, my excellent news. Where is it?"

Laughter and chuckles transpired around the table. Perry scratched a chin. "You know Ken Hobgoolian?"

"Only from fundraisers. The guy's a devious creep."

Said Perry, "Well, the party thinks Senate 2 is long overdue for a change. Naturally, Hobgoolian won't take a hint and retire."

Hollinger pursed his lips. "They'll have to pry him out."

Perry and Brandy exchanged smiles. Perry continued, "The party intends to primary Hobgoolian."

Eyebrows raised, Hollinger said, "He'll hate that."

Perry's mismatched teeth showed. "In fact, Sacramento is considering the young, dynamic District Attorney of Sea Otter Bay to primary Kenneth Hobgoolian. Congratulations, Mr. State Senator."

"Holy shit," said Marcuse. "I mean, holy freaking shit."

"Congrats, boss," said Brandy, beaming.

"I've run the numbers," said Perry. "Hobgoolian's support is slipping. The last few cycles he's been phoning it in. The district is primed for new blood. Oh, and for now, don't say anything. We don't want to give Hobgoolian a chance to muddy you up."

Hollinger pushed away his plate. "We can turn over a few rocks ourselves."

"It's not worth it," said Perry. "The numbers are in your favor."

Hollinger pointed a fork at Brandy. "Dream up something anyway: racism, child trafficking, a conservative uncle."

Brandy giggled. "Working on it."

Outside, ambulances wailed, hauling a rising harvest of shot, stabbed, and mangled to Sea Otter Bay Memorial Hospital.

En route to the office after lunch, Hollinger called his wife Ketta from the back seat of his official SUV. "Well, baby, you're talking to the next state senator from our district."

Ketta squealed. "That is so absolutely hot. But Hobgoolian's held the seat practically forever."

Hollinger chuckled. "His numbers suck. He's dead and doesn't know it yet."

Behind the wheel, a sullen young cop pretended not to hear.

That evening Hollinger passed through the guarded gates and high ivy-covered walls of exclusive Sea Otter Bay Estates. Back home, he kissed a proud Ketta, hugged his nine-year-old daughter, then changed into workout gear. Into the summer dusk, Hollinger commenced his nightly half-hour run along the surf of a private beach. As usual, Marcuse brought along Horkheimer, the family's yappy Boston Terrier. Leash in hand, sea scent filling his nostrils, Marcuse Hollinger ran across the doughy sand of the surf line, grinning to the gentle thunder of the surf.

The next week started out well.

Early Monday morning, following handball, Hollinger attended a breakfast at the Golden Anchor Yacht Club. He received an award for his actions in dealing with small craft graffiti. At the podium, Hollinger proclaimed, "People predicted disaster when I announced my Compassion Not Cops program. And though our police leadership was multicultural and diverse, they were still police. And when you're a cop hammer, every problem looks like a criminal nail."

Laughter, applause.

"Now that 95 percent of the police department is defunded, our trained Equity and Wellness Facilitators are responding to all calls. In time, jails will become yoga and art studios, reminders of a darker era. Remember that smart, thoughtful policies are the hallmark of an engaged community. And I'm here to tell you that today, this day, Sea Otter Bay IS an engaged community.

Death Honk

Applause, cheers, and whistles.

On Tuesday, Hollinger met in his office with a reporter for the online news site *Bay Area Gazette*. A brash, contrarian publication, the *Gazette* was simultaneously dismissed and read by everyone. From her disheveled appearance, middle-aged reporter Terri Ernest appeared to have dressed herself while falling off a bridge. Hollinger greeted her and agreed that the interview was on-the-record. In preparation, Hollinger had removed his jacket and rolled up his sleeves, instructing his assistant to pile case files on his desk.

Tapping a finger on the polished oak desktop, Hollinger said, "Our system is broken. A new structure is needed."

"How does that help a deliveryman cracked over the head by a crystal meth addict?"

"It's not individuals but the justice system that needs a complete overhaul."

"Two days ago, on Harbor Road, a tweaker smashed a brick over the head of a UPS driver. The victim is still in a coma. The tweaker was released as part of your no-cash-bail policy. Any comment?"

"The real victim was the person who needed drug treatment."

"And the UPS driver?"

"A tragedy."

"Since you became district attorney, property crime has increased over forty-five percent, violent crime is up fourteen percent, and Sea Otter Bay leads the state in thefts from vehicles. Shouldn't you bring back some police?"

"Law enforcement punishes the poor and unfortunate. I'm trying to change that."

"The streets are a minefield of rats, needles, and human feces. Your unionized EWF teams are useless. What about the property and security of average citizens?"

"By dealing with larger issues, we are making them safer."

"There's a campaign to recall you. Any comment?"

"A nothing-burger, without traction; it's designed to return us to the tried-and-failed policies of the past."

Marcuse Hollinger then deftly praised his new program of Release Vans. As part of reimagining public safety, Release Vans cruised the streets of Sea Otter Bay, providing mentally ill homeless men a safe space to masturbate.

Terri Ernest munched on her Nicorette. "There was an incident last week on Sutton Street of a homeless man following a mother home and pleasuring himself the whole way. Any comment?"

"I reject single incidents inflated to appear systemic. That is the slimy tactic of goons and political hucksters."

"Gun sales are through the roof. Do you see that as a comment on your policies?"

"Blind, hapless street justice will not be tolerated. Studies show it doesn't work and places children and the elderly at risk."

Finally, pleading another meeting, Hollinger ushered Terri Ernest out. He dialed Brandy. "The interview sucked. Call the Gazette editor and bitch loudly about reporter bias."

"Working on it."

At his private gym on Wednesday morning, Hollinger mentioned the primary to his handball partner. A wealthy stockbroker with many influential clients, the man congratulated Marcuse and swore secrecy.

Thursday turned out to be long and unpleasant.

Marcuse Hollinger chaired a tense stakeholder's meeting that included the director of the new and opaque Justice Force, Media Relations, and the Commissioner of Social Services. In the Hall of Justice conference room, Hollinger exploded. "For God's sake, you people make over six-figures a year plus bonuses and benefits. Why can't I get any freaking help with these EWF teams?"

The balding Commissioner of Social Services raised a pen in the air. He believed his shaved head made him appear dashing. Others felt he looked like a Marvel villain.

"Defunding the police department before our new programs were in place was, perhaps, a bit preemptive."

Media Relations, a young woman with blue-tinged hair, nose rings, and a communication degree from Evergreen College, chimed in. "But great national press. Groundbreaking. We were able to leverage that into the Mayor's big NPR interview."

Hollinger glared at her. "How in bubbling hell does that help me today? Oh, and Terri Ernest from the *Bay Area Gazette* is officially radioactive. Pushy, blunt cow. She acted as if I were an employee or something. Did you call her editor and bitch about reporter bias?"

"At top volume."

"At least something is going right."

Turning to a short, round, dark-skinned woman festooned with turquoise jewelry, Hollinger snapped, "Okay, Justice Force, why are the EWF teams so absolutely fouled up?"

The woman gestured, initiating a soft chain reaction of clicking turquoise jewelry. "A certain unruly element knows EWFs are unarmed therapists and social workers. So, these unruly elements call 911 with bogus mental health issues or domestic violence calls. When our EWF teams arrive, they're robbed of radios, wallets, and cell phones. Several have been beaten."

The social services commissioner added, "The union is howling. They want to pull everyone off the job until team safety can be guaranteed."

The Justice Force Director pleaded, "You can't replace experience with politics. Couldn't we add a cop to the teams? Just for now. Just until EWF finds its feet."

Hollinger plopped down into an ergonomic chair, lips curling in sarcasm. "Brilliant. Scintillating. Send the police back out on calls? I'll look like a drooling idiot."

The Commissioner of Social Services glanced at his reflection in the office window glass and smiled at Hollinger. "How about your DA investigators? Most of them are retired cops and sheriffs. Send one of them along. It's not so obvious."

Marcuse grimaced. "Good idea. But I fired all the old investigators. They've been replaced with sociology graduates from Stanford."

Media Relations added, "Favorable press in Palo Alto.

A rattle of turquoise. "At least let the EWF carry tasers."

Hollinger threw up both arms. "Why not AR-15s? Why not rocket launchers?"

Back-and-forth they went. Finally, near the end of the workday, it was decided to equip all Equity and Wellness Facilitators with non-irritating pepper spray.

That Friday at 7:09, Hollinger arrived back at Sea Otter Bay Estates, stressed out and primed for the weekend. After kissing-hugging-changing, he embarked on his evening run. Forty-one minutes later, a yapping Horkheimer returned home, leash dragging in the sand. Ketta scanned the beach for her husband. Nothing but the cry of gulls.

Leaving her daughter with the au pair, a concerned Ketta searched the private beach. No husband. She questioned neighbors. Nothing. Finally, an anxious Ketta Hollinger called 911. Because they were on a union meal break, twenty-seven minutes passed before an EWF team arrived.

A sharp clash erupted between the Equity and Wellness Facilitators and Ketta over subsequent procedure. The EWF duo believed their mission was to psychologically comfort Ketta over her loss. Ketta, however, felt they should be out searching for her husband. Soothing words of emotional support were drowned out by loud deprecating insults. A squeaky chew toy was hurled; non-irritating pepper spray brandished. Retreating to their electric car, the EWF placed several phone and radio calls. They sought to discover if the defunded police department still retained any detectives.

In the meantime, the District Attorney of Sea Otter Bay remained missing.

***

In an eerie androgynous voice, the robot said to Hollinger, "Repeat: 'I'm a silly goose.'"

"You want me to say that?"

"Then make a goose noise."

Despite the situation, Hollinger's lips curled. "You're kidding me."

"Repeat: 'I'm a silly goose.' Then honk like a goose."

"What happens after that?"

"You go home."

"How do I know I can trust you?"

The robot spun around, heading back to the darkness.

"Wait. Please. Okay. But you're risking prison for something dumb. Have you considered that?"

Reversing itself, the robot backed up, spun around, stopping near the toes of Hollinger's ASIC.

"Repeat: 'I'm a silly goose.'"

"Could you tell me why you want me to say that?"

"Repeat 'I'm a silly goose.' Then honk like a goose.'"

"Geese don't honk. They make some unusual avian sound."

"You must honk as best you can."

Silence stretched out. Weird voice. Spoken elsewhere and filtered, or the programmed voice of the robot? Say something stupid, make a stupid noise, then go home. Really?

Hollinger cleared his throat. "Listen to me. This is political, right? I'm on camera. You want some tiny snippet of embarrassing footage to loop online and hope it goes viral. It won't work. People don't believe things acquired under duress. I've met the Zuckerbergs. Nice people. They'll censor it from their social media platforms. I'll be a sympathetic figure. You're risking a long stretch in prison for lame trolling that can't possibly help you."

"Repeat 'I'm a silly goose.' Then honk like a goose.'"

"Release me now. I swear, there'll be no investigation."

A high-pitched whine. Extending upward, the robot's solitary arm clamped onto Hollinger's left pinky finger. A sudden right twist and Hollinger's finger snapped with a wet pop.

Hollinger lost track of time. In pain, he was hungry and thirsty and needed to go to the bathroom. Yet his entire existence was reduced to pleasing a cheap robot with a limited vocabulary. After a series of failed takes, the robot broke his right pinky finger. In desperation, Hollinger resorted to the same caring, sincere voice he used when deceiving his daughter or the voters. He finally said, 'I'm a silly goose' to the robot's satisfaction. But the mandatory goose honk proved impossible, incomprehensible. Marcuse hollered and cawed and shrieked. His throat grew raw.

"I need water."

"Say it better."

"I've done all I can. I don't care what happens."

The metal arm reached for Hollinger's groin.

"Let me try something different."

Marcuse Hollinger erupted in a long, high-pitched bray laced with frustration, anxiety, and fury. When he finished, the robot sat quietly for so long that Hollinger whimpered from tension. Without any further communication, the robot trundled out of sight. The overhead light winked out. Hollinger sat alone, his throat burning. At some point, he dropped into an exhausted sleep.

Lips dry and cracked, little fingers throbbing in pain, Hollinger awoke. Had a bird twittered outside? He felt it might now be daylight. They'd be searching for him. Ketta would see to that. He'd been kidnapped off a private beach on a private estate with cameras everywhere. In addition, everyone carried a cell phone with a camera. Surely, a neighbor, au pair, governess, maid, or private security guard caught some of the incident on film.

What if the robot had lied? What if he were left in the chair to slowly starve?

Someone must've entered the room from behind. Another sharp sting to Marcuse Hollinger's neck. More blackness.

Hollinger awoke Saturday evening in a Sea Otter Bay homeless encampment. Disoriented, with pained little fingers twisted at strange angles, Hollinger noticed the ASICS had been stolen off his feet. Seeking help, Marcuse roamed the frenzied unruly sidewalks. At one point, he jumped aside to avoid stepping on a syringe, hopping into a pile of human feces.

***

In his favorite upscale eatery, Marcuse Hollinger ignored a bowl of too-brothy clam chowder. Holding a spoon was difficult with splints on both fingers. In any case, Hollinger's appetite had suffered since his release from captivity four days earlier. Saturday evening, legs covered with flea bites, Hollinger had staggered into a rescue mission. An amazed priest recognized the District Attorney from television. Hollinger borrowed the man's cell phone and called 911. But the EWF responded to the wrong location, where their vehicle was carjacked. Hollinger called his wife. An ecstatic Ketta rushed to collect him.

Sipping a Pierre Sparr Riesling with notes of grapefruit and green melon, the District Attorney watched a nearby freeway. A colorful homeless tent had caught fire, flames snapping upward toward the freeway above.

"It looks bad," said Perry.

"Worse than that," added Brandy. "That video was up and viral before you were found."

"Why are we still insisting I not make a statement?"

Perry shook his head. "The truth makes you sound loony."

Brandy recited, "I was kidnapped, then tortured by a robot who broke both my pinky fingers until I said, 'I'm a silly goose.'" She answered a text. "We're marginally better off if we keep messaging that the video is fake news."

Hollinger's voice rose as he raised his splinted fingers. "Are these fake?" Perry and Brandy muttered their 'nos,' tones sympathetic. Hollinger added, "Now, on top of that, I'm being recalled? How does that happen?"

"Suppressed anger and discontent finding a catalyst," said Perry. "Once the video went viral, all the fence-sitters jumped. They've got real momentum now."

"Hobgoolian," whispered Hollinger, voice distant as speaking under hypnosis.

Brandy adjusted her cat-eyeglasses. "Or a couple of fired cops with a sick sense of humor. Let's face it, no disrespect, but as long as they didn't take you across state lines, who would catch them?"

Hollinger stared at the freeway as a second tent caught fire. From reports, he knew the homeless cooked with propane tanks issued to them by the city. In addition to incendiary accidents, the homeless also set revenge fires over drug deals gone sour.

Perry said, "Sacramento is pretending they never heard of you."

Leaning forward, Brandy touched Hollinger's forearm. "It was that godawful yell. I mean, so bizarre, so haunting.

Hollinger said, "It was a goose honk. That's what the robot made me say."

Perry selected a chin to scratch. "Sounded like a devil goose. It still resonates."

Another tent caught fire. Then a third. Sirens sounded in the distance. Hollinger watched as black smoke roiled upward, coiling into a cloudless summer sky.

Notes

A print version of "Dagon and Jill" first appeared in Stygian Publications *Necrotic Tissue*, Issue Number 13, under the name John P. McCann on January 21, 2011. The story was again printed in *Necrotic Tissue: Best Of Anthology* published on October 16, 2011. Wildside Press included the story in their ebook, *Cthulhu Mythos Megapack,* released April 17, 2012.

Indigo Mosaic Press published "Bummed Out," under the name John P. McCann in a print anthology titled *The Darkness Within*, released December 17, 2012.

"Mark of the Bruja" debuted in the Soteira Press print anthology *Horror USA: California*, published December 13, 2019.

"Fresh Ideas" first appeared online under the name John P. McCann at *Every Day Fiction*, published May 24, 2010. Subsequently, a print version graced *Every Day Publishing's Best of Every Day Fiction Three*. Portable Press printed the story in *Uncle John's Bathroom Reader Presents Flush Fiction* on August 15, 2012.

A vastly different Flash Fiction version of "Death Honk" under the name John P. McCann was published online at the *Journal of Microliterature* on August 15, 2010.

Acknowledgements

One constant over the last decade has been the keen eyes of Ken Segall and Dan Hoffman. Beta readers come and go, but these bookish men remain, ever ready to peruse whatever prose I've tapped out.

Thanks to fellow writer Dutch Heckman for his friendship. He's lent a willing ear to my writerly woes at the best coffee shop a fellow could ask for: Foxy's in Glendale, California.

Also, a nod to Bernadette Murphy's Thursday morning writers' group. Under Bernadette's guidance, I strove to learn Elmore Leonard's classic admonition to leave out "the parts that people tend to skip."

Cover art courtesy of Brandi Doane McCann at eBook Cover Designs.

Wonderlist proofed the final manuscript while Joy McCann read five of these stories before I originally submitted them. As good an editor as one might find, Joy's as fine a wife as one might wed.

About the Author

Mac's short fiction has appeared in venues such as *The Best of Every Day Fiction Three* and *The Cthulhu Mythos Mega Pack*. A former marathon runner, Mac lives in the hills above Los Angeles with his wife. When not watching neighbors flee the once Golden State, Mac types away on book two of his *Hallow Mass* horror trilogy.

Learn more at his author website at
https://jpmac.squarespace.com.

About the Publisher

This book is indie-published, so we remind you that reviews are pivotal in keeping our small business alive. If you enjoyed this book, we strongly urge you to review it on Amazon or Goodreads so we can stay visible. Even a single sentence will help us out.

If you review this book in print or for an online website, blog, vlog, or podcast, please drop us a line so we can highlight your mention on social media.

— Joy McCann
Production Manager
joy.mccann@gmail.com
Cornerstone Media, La Cañada, California

Made in the USA
Las Vegas, NV
13 February 2021